RETURN
FROM
WITCH MOUNTAIN

Westminster Press Books by
ALEXANDER KEY

Return from Witch Mountain

Jagger the Dog from Elsewhere

The Magic Meadow

The Preposterous Adventures
of Swimmer

The Strange White Doves

Flight to the Lonesome Place

The Incredible Tide

The Golden Enemy

Escape to Witch Mountain

Mystery of the Sassafras Chair

The Forgotten Door

Rivets and Sprockets

RETURN FROM WITCH MOUNTAIN

by

ALEXANDER KEY

Based on
Walt Disney Productions'
motion picture screenplay
written by

MALCOLM MARMORSTEIN

Based on characters created by
Alexander Key

THE WESTMINSTER PRESS
Philadelphia

Book Design by Dorothy Alden Smith

First edition

Published by The Westminster Press ®

Philadelphia, Pennsylvania

PRINTED IN THE UNITED STATES OF AMERICA

9 8 7 6 5 4 3 2 1

Library of Congress Cataloging in Publication Data

Key, Alexander, 1904–
    Return from Witch Mountain.

    Sequel to Escape to Witch Mountain.
    SUMMARY: Tia and Tony's visit to Earth is disrupted
when Tony is kidnapped by a power-crazed doctor wishing
to use the boy's special powers for his own evil purposes.
    [1. Science fiction] I. Marmorstein, Malcolm. Return
from Witch Mountain. II. Title.
PZ7.K51Re   [Fic]   77-26992
ISBN 0-664-32630-7

To the many fans of
Tony and Tia

CONTENTS

I

VENTURE

UNCLE BENÉ, a very accomplished pilot in spite of his years and snowy beard, set their craft down neatly and exactly on the fifty-yard line of the empty Rose Bowl. Then, smiling like a diminutive Santa Claus, he touched the button that opened the cabin portal.

"Here we are, folks!" he announced.

Tony and his sister, Tia, scrambled out quickly with their bags. Uncle Bené followed, and they started along the edge of the field to the gate. Tia moved eagerly, pale hair flying, dark eyes bright, for ahead was all the excitement of a glittering new city to explore. But Tony, who had the often worrisome gift of being able to see things before they happened, had sudden misgivings. There was excitement ahead, surely. And there was also trouble. He could feel it coming.

As they approached the gate Tony wished they had gone to the beach instead, or even stayed home at Witch Mountain. After all their work at home, learning to use abilities they didn't know they possessed, and helping their people build up their new community, Uncle Bené had arranged this as a sort of vacation. And Uncle Bené was the last person on the planet Earth Tony wanted to offend.

Tony could never forget those terrible days, when, as refugees from a beautiful world now destroyed, they had reached this curious planet, only to become separated from their people. But for Uncle Bené, they would never have lived to see their own kind again, and join them at their new home. The most wonderful part was that Uncle Bené, who they thought had died while trying to save them, had managed to live. It was truly a miracle.

Tony returned to the present as they reached the gate. He watched Uncle Bené try to open it.

"It's locked," he said. "Come on!"

Using energy in the way he had been taught at Witch Mountain, he rose easily into the air, bag in hand, and started to move over the gate.

"Tony!" Uncle Bené said sharply. "Come back here!"

"What is it?" Tony asked, coming to a stop.

"All the way back," Uncle Bené ordered.

Tony gave a little shrug and came easily down to the ground.

"You mustn't do things like that," Uncle Bené said worriedly. "You might frighten someone. Besides, it isn't wise to draw attention to ourselves. Earth people don't understand about energizing matter."

Tia said, "We're supposed to be like ordinary Earth kids."

"So," Uncle Bené went on, "don't energize unless it's absolutely necessary."

"But it's necessary," Tony argued. "The gate's locked."

10

Uncle Bené glanced at Tia and gave a slight nod.

Tia studied the gate a moment, then focused her attention on the lock. In the past she had been forced to touch a lock and give it a physical jerk before she could open it. But the Witch Mountain way was far better. The mind did it all.

The rusty old lock, with a squeak and a groan, unlocked itself. Creaking, the big gate swung open.

The three of them went through, then Tia turned and energized the gate again. Obligingly it closed, and the lock relocked itself. She couldn't help a quick smile of delight. This was great fun!

Uncle Bené said, "If the Earth kids can live here without energizing, perhaps you can too, for a few days." He put his arms about them and they began walking toward the parking area where a shiny new taxi stood waiting.

The motor was running, Tony noticed, and the cabby was pacing irritably back and forth, checking his watch and shaking his head as if he had been waiting far too long. But at the sudden sight of them the cabby hopped into his machine, slammed it in reverse, backed rapidly, and screeched to a stop just in front of them, blocking the way.

"Hey," he demanded, "you the party what I'm supposed to pick up?"

Uncle Bené nodded. "Yes. But just the children."

The cabby hopped out and opened the rear door, then snatched the luggage Tony and Tia were carrying. He was a thin, impatient character who wore a jump suit with various patches sewed upon it, as if he fancied himself to be more of a race driver than a cabby.

"Meter's runnin'," he snapped. "Hop in, hop in, hop in!"

As Tia and Tony got inside he opened the taxi trunk and stowed their luggage. "Name's Eddie," he continued. "I been waitin' here forever. People are supposed to wait for taxis . . . not taxis for people."

"We are exactly on time," Uncle Bené told him.

"Kind of a strange time an' place to be makin' a pickup," Eddie flung back. "I mean . . . if you're here for the next game, it's in three months!"

"We have seats on the fifty-yard line," Uncle Bené said mildly, winking at Tony.

Eddie, as if sensing something foreign here, looked him up and down curiously—it was the same look strangers often gave members of the Witch Mountain community—then slammed the trunk closed and got back into the driver's seat. Impatiently he gunned the motor.

Uncle Bené gave him a slip of paper, and said, "Take the children to this address. They'll pay you when you arrive."

"This is a big fare," Eddie reminded him. "If them kids is gonna pay me, I hope they know I get a big tip."

"They know," Uncle Bené assured him, and turned to Tony and Tia. "Everything has been worked out for you," he went on. "Stick to the schedule, remember what I told you, and have a wonderful time. I'll see you Friday."

He gave each of them a good-bye kiss through the open window, then stepped back quickly as the impatient Eddie sent the taxi forward.

For the next twenty minutes Tony's attention was

12

divided between Eddie and his wild driving, and the uncertainty that lay ahead. The uncertainty had nothing to do with the concerts, museum visits, and other educational plums with which their vacation was liberally sprinkled. He had a feeling, in fact, that they were going to miss the educational plums entirely. Something was going to happen. And Eddie, he suddenly realized, was part of it.

For a moment, as he watched Eddie hunched over the wheel, honking the horn and weaving madly in and out of the traffic, he was afraid they might be involved in an accident. For safety's sake he wondered if he and Tia hadn't better energize. But before he could mention it to her the taxi whipped around a corner, tires screeching, and all at once the motor began to sputter.

"W-what's that?" Eddie cried, shocked. "What's happening?"

"You're out of gas," Tony informed him, after concentrating quickly on the motor.

"What are you . . . crazy? Look at the gas gauge! It's—" Eddie gulped, then gave a despairing groan. "Empty!"

The taxi, motor completely dead, coasted to a stop at the curb. They all got out, and Eddie took a gas can from the trunk.

"It was all that waitin' I hadda do for you," he grumbled. "I'll run down the street to a gas station. You're costin' me a lota dough. You sure better make the tip worth it."

Tony, frowning, watched Eddie hurry away, the gas can swinging from his hand. Tony shook his head and started to turn back to Tia. At that moment something flashed through his mind. It was a hazy view of a falling figure.

Even Tia reacted to it, for she said, "What was that?"

"I—I'm not sure . . . but something's going to happen to someone . . . near here."

"Let's try to help," Tia said quickly.

"You'd better wait for the driver. I'll go."

He closed his eyes a moment, concentrating, then started up the street toward the nearest corner. "I think it came from over in that direction . . . "

"Hurry back," Tia called as he turned the corner. "And remember what Uncle Bené said."

• • •

If Tony had seen the long black car with the tinted windows that, some minutes earlier, had parked on a side street ahead, he would have felt instantly that there was something sinister about it, and he would have wanted nothing to do with its occupants. But he was focusing only the falling figure in his mind—a figure that had not yet begun to fall, but surely would in a very short time.

Earlier, when the black car had stopped, its three occupants got out and stood looking speculatively at the tall old structures on either side. They were in a run-down area bordering the slums, and not many of the buildings were occupied.

The car's driver, a hard-eyed and muscular young man the others called Sickle, glanced at the woman and said, "How's this place, Aunt Letha?"

Letha Wedge peered about uncomfortably and

14

pursed her thin lips. She was one of yesterday's aristo-crats, and her expensive clothing had once been fashion-able. Time had lined her still-handsome face and made it eaglelike and predatory. She nodded, and looked at the man beside her.

"This seems like the perfect test site. Little traffic, and low real estate value. What do you think, Victor?"

Dr. Victor Gannon, who was not unknown in scien-tific circles, was studying the tallest building with nar-rowed, calculating eyes. In his square hands was a com-pact electronic control unit, which he was holding carefully. He grunted, and said shortly, "It's adequate."

Sickle's tight mouth twitched nervously. "Then let's get it over with." He pointed to something behind his ear. It was a small electronic receptor attached to his head. "Is this thing all right?"

Dr. Gannon peered at it closely, tested it with a few taps of his finger, and nodded gravely. "It's ready."

Letha Wedge said, "What do you want him to do this time?"

The scientist pointed to the tallest building across the street. "I want him to climb that fire escape to the absolute top."

Letha Wedge gasped, and Sickle's mouth came open.

"Hey, wait a minute," Sickle muttered. He seemed to have contracted a chill. "This is as high as I go. You want me to break somebody's leg . . . just tell me how many pieces. But don't ask me to climb up there."

Dr. Gannon's eyebrows went up. "Why not?"

"Because . . . I'm afraid of heights. I'll get dizzy and . . . fall."

"It's true, Victor," Letha Wedge hastened to say.

15

"He has acrophobia, among other things. Find a different test for him."

Dr. Gannon shrugged. "Acrophobia won't be a problem with my device. Start climbing, Sickle."

"I—I'll do anything you say, Doctor, . . . but I won't do that!"

He began backing away in fright, but Dr. Gannon raised the control unit in his hand and suddenly switched it on. Sickle stopped on the instant. His body went rigid and all expression left his face. More than anything he resembled a dummy in a clothing store window.

Dr. Gannon smiled. "Sickle," he began, speaking into the control unit and pointing across the street, "I command you to climb that fire escape. When you reach the top, you will turn and look down. You will not be affected by height. Go now."

Sickle turned and, moving like a sleepwalker, crossed the street to the building.

"It's working!" the doctor whispered, showing excitement for the first time. "It's working!"

"So it seems," Letha Wedge said uneasily. "But you're risking his life. He's my nephew, my only living relative, the only one I can leave my bankruptcy to."

"That's what experimentation is all about, Letha."

"But we can't afford to lose him!"

"I'm the only one you can't afford to lose," the doctor reminded her, holding up the unit. "Can't you see I'm in complete control of his mind? He no longer has fear or memory or will. He can only carry out my commands. I've done it!" he added triumphantly.

Letha Wedge clenched her long bony hands. Why did

16

Victor have to be so coldly calculating? It was a frightening side of him. But she needed him and would have to go along with what he did.

Her hands tightened as she watched Sickle climb steadily up the fire escape. Every movement of his arms and legs was curiously mechanical, as if he had turned into a robot. When he reached a high ledge her heart contracted and she said suddenly, "That's enough! Bring him down, Victor. He has the car keys."

Dr. Gannon ignored her. "Sickle," he ordered into the unit, "turn to the right. Balance yourself . . . and walk along the ledge. Now!"

"Victor—no!"

Still the doctor ignored her. She watched in a sort of horror as her nephew, mechanically obeying instructions, began to walk along the narrow ledge. All at once she could stand it no longer. She whirled and clutched Dr. Gannon's arm.

"Stop him!"

He shook his head. "I won't stop in the middle of a test. I'm going to prove to you the extent to which I can control the human mind."

"You've already proved it! I believe you. Don't make him go any farther!"

"I can make him do anything I want!" the doctor told her, excitement rising in him. "It works perfectly! I'm in complete control of him! I could have ten men up there—"

"I'll bring him down myself!" Letha Wedge cried in desperation. "Give me that!"

She snatched at the control unit. He struggled to keep it. The thing flew out of their hands and fell to the hard

17

paving, throwing up a shower of sparks. From it came a beeping signal as a red light began to flash.

They scrambled for the unit, and Dr. Gannon managed to snatch it up. "Look what you've done!" he cried, flicking the switches. "Sickle!" he spoke hoarsely into the unit. "Sickle! Stop! I command you to stop!"

Sickle, high above them, paid no attention. When the unit dropped he had seemed momentarily affected, but now he proceeded ahead, moving steadily toward the open end of the ledge.

Dr. Gannon tried desperately to use the damaged unit, then gave it up and gasped, "He's out of control!"

"Sickle!" Letha Wedge shouted. "Sickle! Go back! Go back!" She stared in horror as Sickle, without a break in his stride, walked off the end of the ledge and plunged toward the street.

A sob broke from her and she turned away, hands over her face.

2

MIND CONTROL

TONY was hurrying up a side street toward another corner when his sharp ears picked up Letha Wedge's agonized voice ahead. At the same moment he became aware of Tia, who was waiting by the taxi, calling to him telepathically.

"Tony, have you found it?"

"Not yet," he called back. "But I'm very close."

He began to run. But as he rounded the corner he stopped short, looking upward, and saw the silent figure of Sickle plunging downward.

Sickle was hardly thirty feet from the paving when Tony sighted him. Instantly his mind reached forth and caught Sickle, degravitating him so that he hung suspended over the street.

Dr. Gannon, watching, was completely aghast. "Look! Look!" he cried to Letha Wedge. She refused to turn, and he spun her around and pointed.

At the sight of her nephew motionless overhead she was momentarily speechless. Then she managed to ask, "Is—is your control unit having some sort of side effect?"

"It's not the control," the doctor said hoarsely. "It's that—that—*boy!*"

While the two of them stared, openmouthed, Tony energized Sickle and began easing him over to his own side of the street.

"It—it's miraculous!" Letha Wedge gasped.

"There are no miracles," Dr. Gannon informed her. "Only scientific answers for everything."

"Then explain what we've just seen!"

"We've seen a force . . . counteract the basic physical law of gravity. Counteract it on demand."

"*What* force?" she asked.

He looked up the street and saw Tony, rigid with concentration. Gannon's eyes widened.

"A force that centers around . . . that boy."

"Victor, I *don't* know what you're saying."

"I know exactly what I'm saying—and seeing! Molecular mobilization." Then the doctor said softly, coldly, "I need that boy . . . need him desperately!"

Letha Wedge studied him apprehensively. Her eyes narrowed. "Now just a minute . . ."

The doctor gave her a withering look. She nodded.

The two approached Tony, who had guided Sickle to the paving and now was trying to balance him on his feet.

"Brilliant!" said Dr. Gannon. "Brilliant!"

The doctor took Sickle by the elbow, saying, "Poor fellow, he's in shock," and guided him behind Tony as if leading him to the car. Tony's attention was immediately taken up by a smiling Letha Wedge, who grasped his hand warmly.

"Young man," she began, "congratulations on a fan-

20

tastic—er—whatever it was you did. It was absolutely heroic! You deserve a reward!" She released his hand and began fumbling in her bag.

Tony shook his head. "I don't need—"

He was unable to finish. Something stung him in the back and the world began to slide away from him. Even so, in a swift reaction he was able to turn his head and catch a fleeting glimpse of Dr. Gannon stepping away from him, a hypodermic needle in his hand. Then everything went black, and he fell forward into Letha Wedge's arms.

• • •

As Dr. Gannon thrust the hypodermic into Tony's back, Tia, waiting by the taxi, had a sharp reaction. It was almost as if she, too, had been jabbed with a needle.

"Tony!" she called. "Tony! What happened?"

She waited, fear creeping through her, then called again, "Where are you? Tony! Tony!"

Her fear rose, bordering on panic. Tony was in trouble. If he couldn't answer, he must be hurt. She called once more and forced herself to wait while she listened. But all at once she could stand it no longer and began running in the direction Tony had taken.

If she had remained by the taxi a few more seconds, she might have seen Eddie hurrying back with a can of gasoline. But she turned the corner just before the cabby came hurrying up behind her.

Several minutes later, sure that she had covered the area where Tony must have been, she hastened back to the spot where the taxi had parked. As she rounded the

21

corner she was just in time to see Eddie driving furiously away.

Tia cried out and ran frantically for a little way until she saw the uselessness of it. Then she stopped and leaned helplessly against the side of a building, wondering what to do.

Her first concern was Tony. How could she find him? Would it help to go to the police? What could she tell them? If she tried to explain how Tony went over to another street to save a person who was falling from a great height, she could imagine what their reaction would be. For one thing they wouldn't believe her, and on top of it she would be in for endless questioning. Who were her parents? Where did she live? And of course she couldn't tell about Witch Mountain, because the quickest and surest way to destroy it would be for the world to know about it.

In her despair she might have weakened and sought help from the police anyway, except that just *talking* the way Earth people did was so tiring and difficult. The natural speech of her own people was ultrasonic, and Earth people, with their poor ears, couldn't even hear it. The most difficult thing she'd ever learned was to talk the way Earth people did, so they could understand her. She envied the easy way Tony had learned.

Tia wished Uncle Bené had given her the address where the taxi was supposed to take them. That would be of some help now, for she knew Tony had it, and the sensible thing would be to go there and wait. But she didn't know the address, so that was that. And except for Uncle Bené, who must be halfway home by now, there were no Witch Mountain people around, so it

22

wouldn't do any good to send out a telepathic call for help. Even if Uncle Bené were only a few miles away, he wouldn't be able to hear her, for his telepathic range was very short.

Tia closed her eyes and fought back the tears that wanted to come. Somehow she'd find Tony, even if she had to do it alone. Perhaps if she just started walking, following her instincts and calling to Tony every few minutes, he'd hear her in time. . . .

• • •

It was a very run-down and depressing part of the city that Tia found herself in late that afternoon. Too exhausted at the moment to go farther, she sat down on a rickety wooden platform beside an abandoned building and tried to ignore the ugliness around her. Again she tried to fight back tears. This time they came, but she brushed them aside fiercely, determined not to be beaten in spite of the way she felt.

Once more she raised her head, preparing to send forth another and, she hoped, a stronger call to Tony, but she was suddenly interrupted by racing footsteps and frantic shouting.

Turning quickly, she saw four boys, all slightly older than herself, running along the edge of the broken paving toward her. From the looks on their faces, their very lives might have been at stake.

"Get off the streets!" the first boy yelled, as he sped past.

"Run!" cried the others. "Hide!"

The last boy, white with fear, managed to gasp, "It's

23

the Golden Goons! Here they come!" He paused briefly, pointed an unsteady finger up the street, and raced onward.

Now Tia saw a group of larger and much tougher-looking boys swing around a corner and come pounding after the first four. In sudden confusion she sprang to her feet. Seeing her, they began to shout in a way that left no doubt in her mind of the sort of treatment she would get if they caught her. She whirled and fled in the direction of the smaller boys.

At the next corner she started to turn left, following two of the smaller boys who were just ahead of her. But she was shocked to see more of the Golden Goons appear from an alleyway, neatly outflanking them. They were forced to swing to the right, where a wrecked and abandoned car lay like a squashed bug near the end of the street.

The car was a trap. Just as they approached it, Tia saw movement behind it and cried out a warning. The frightened four swerved to the right, and raced down a narrow alley just as two more Goons, wearing yellow jackets like the rest, popped up from the wreck and pounded after them.

Too late Tia realized the alley was a dead end. They were neatly caught, and there was no escape.

The Goons, seven of them now, slowed to a walk and advanced in a line, ominously. Several carried sticks. One had a knife, and the largest, a heavily built boy who seemed to be the leader, had brass knuckles on each hand.

The leader grinned suddenly and spat on his brass knuckles. "Okay, guys, let's finish 'em!"

24

There was nowhere to hide except behind the battered garbage cans that filled the end of the alley. The frightened victims, already torn and badly bruised from an earlier attack, huddled behind the cans, clinging to each other defensively.

Tia, confused till now, was all at once furious. She heard one of the smaller boys whimper, "They—they're gonna finish us!" and she looked quickly around for a weapon. Seeing nothing but the garbage cans, she energized one and sent it rolling toward the advancing line.

Faster and faster the can spun. It struck the line of Goons and rolled through them, dumping them head over heels like bowling pins.

The four victims were as surprised as their aggressors. They stared incredulously at Tia, who was standing with clenched hands and outthrust jaw. Suddenly they broke into a cheer and cried out their thanks.

The confused Goons scrambled to their feet. They were not quite sure what had happened, but they were furious that it had happened to them. Closing in, they began moving forward again, and this time it was easy to see that they were out for blood.

Tia had hoped they would go away. Fighting was so stupid, and she hated being placed on the defensive. But something had to be done, and there was no one but herself to do it. Turning quickly, she energized the rest of the garbage cans and tilted them forward like cannons. Abruptly the garbage was fired out of them in a great salvo.

The smaller boys gaped in amazement as their enemies were bombarded. And Tia, weary and upset as she was, could not suppress a giggle. It *was* funny.

25

But not for very long. All too quickly the barrage of garbage ended, the cans being out of ammunition. The bespattered Goons, cursing now and enraged beyond endurance, charged murderously.

The smaller boys huddled behind the cans again and looked helplessly at Tia. There was only one thing left to do. For the second time she energized the garbage cans, so that they shot upward and forward almost as if the smaller boys had thrown them. Turning them so that the open ends faced the enemy, she brought them down over the heads and shoulders of the Goons, and thrust them tight so that those inside could only stagger blindly about, bumping into each other and the alley walls with loud crashes that drowned their muffled cries for help.

It was a wonderful sight for the four former victims to watch, and for delightful seconds they did watch with openmouthed amazement. Then, realizing this was their chance to escape, one of them cried, "Hey, you guys! We'd better split!"

Taking Tia's hands, they dodged past the stumbling Goons and ran out of the alley. Minutes later, after following a winding route that led through broken fences, a burned-out building, down two more alleys, and around a construction site, Tia found herself under a bridge spanning a drainage area.

The four boys stood looking at her with a mixture of adoration and wonder.

"Gee," said one. "Dunno how you did it, but you really saved us from being wiped out."

"You sure did," said another, and added earnestly, "Thanks a lot!"

26

The others thanked her and each shook her hand. Then a short, dark-haired boy asked, "What's your name?"

"Tia," she replied, in the small but audible voice she had worked so hard to acquire.

"I'm Rocky," said the dark-haired boy.

"I'm Muscles," said another, who hardly had a sign of a muscle on his skinny frame.

"Me, I'm Crusher," said the third. He spoke out of the side of his mouth, as if trying to be much tougher than he looked.

"And I'm Dazzler," said the fourth. He added proudly, "We're the Earthquake gang!"

The skinny Muscles asked, "Does that scare you?"

"No," said Tia, with a little shake of her head.

The dark-haired Rocky said, "Mebbe we'd better change our name again. Gotta have a name that scares."

Crusher, who had been looking at her curiously, said, "Hey, how did you do what you done?"

"Oh, I didn't really do anything," she told them.

Dazzler asked, "You a magician or something?"

"No," she said, smiling faintly.

"Wanna join our gang?" Crusher asked.

"I'm sorry," she replied. "I'm looking for someone. Thank you anyway."

"Oh, sure," grumbled Muscles. "I guess you're like the rest of 'em. You musta heard we're a nothin' gang." He seemed depressed by the thought.

Dazzler said quickly, "We ain't always gonna be nothin'."

"Someday," said Muscles, "we're gonna be the

toughest. We're gonna take over this whole territory!"

"Yeah," said Crusher. "Someday they're gonna run when they see us comin' down the block. They're gonna shiver when they hear our name."

Tia looked from one to the other. "You don't understand," she told them. "I like you all. It's just that I'm trying to find my brother."

"Your brother?" said Rocky. "What gang does he belong to?"

"He doesn't belong to any gang."

"Never heard of a guy who didn't belong to a gang," Crusher said, shaking his head.

"But you see," Tia hastened to add, "we're just visitors here. Tony and I got separated. He—he went to look at something—and didn't come back. I—I'm sure something's happened to him. I've got to find him!"

They were all silent a moment, looking at her sympathetically. Then Muscles said, "If anybody can find him, we can. We know this town inside out."

Tia caught her breath. "Would—would you help me?"

Dazzler grinned. "Sure we will! You done us a big favor. Now we'll do one for you."

3

SEARCH

THEY STARTED out eagerly enough that afternoon, Tia with rising hope, and the Earthquake gang as if they were secret agents caught up in an exciting undercover job. In the beginning it didn't go too badly. The boys were clever enough to unravel Tia's earlier wandering and locate the spot where the taxi had run out of gas. Then they covered the probable area where Tony had vanished, asking questions, poking through empty buildings, and checking dark alleys for signs of possible skulduggery. But from then on the search rather went to pieces. It was finally climaxed by an unpleasant encounter with the law in the form of Mr. Yokomoto, the truant officer.

It happened suddenly, just as they reached a corner and at a moment when everyone's spirits were at a low ebb. As they started to step off the curb, a minibus cut abruptly in front of them and stopped, blocking their path.

The boys yelped in surprise and dismay as the driver, a burly little man with a look of bulldog determination on his face, leaped out quickly. He was around the

29

minibus in a flash, hands extended to catch them.

"Okay, kids!" he snapped. "It's all over! Get in!"

"It's Yokomoto!" Crusher yelled. "Let's get outa here!"

The Earthquakes dodged and ran, dragging Tia with them. The burly little man gave chase, angrily ordering them back. But he was gradually left behind as they scrambled through fences and made their way down an alley.

"Who is he?" Tia asked, when she had got her breath.

"Our w-worst enemy!" Crusher panted, and Dazzler added, "Worse than the Golden Goons!"

Muscles said, "He's the truant officer! He's tryin' to make us go to school!"

Tia caught a final glimpse of the officer far behind them, angrily shaking his fist and shouting, "I'll get you yet!"

In the safety of the next alley the Earthquakes stopped to rest while they considered the next move. Twilight had come, and Tia, who had been hunting for Tony all day, was nearly exhausted. More than that, she was as discouraged as she had ever been. Had she been alone she would have broken down and cried. In her concern for Tony she was desperately hungry and she hadn't even considered where she was going to spend the night. In the back of her mind was the awful thought that Tony had been terribly hurt in an accident and might even be dead. But she kept thrusting the thought away, as far away as she could, so that she wouldn't lose the hope that kept her going.

"That Tony," Crusher mumbled, "he sure made himself scarce. I can't figure . . ."

"That Tony ain't nowhere," Rocky said dispiritedly.

Muscles said, "I can't think of no place else to look."

"He must've evaporated," Crusher muttered.

"You dummy!" said Dazzler. "People don't evaporate! Milk evaporates!"

Muscles shook his head. "It's gettin' sorta late," he said wearily. He looked at Tia in sudden concern, then said, "Hey, guys, don'tcha think we better walk her home?"

"Yeah," said Dazzler. "Where d'ya live, Tia?"

"I—I'm supposed to stay at a hotel," she said, trying not to sound as dejected as she felt. "But—but I don't know which one."

"You can stay at our secret hideout," Dazzler offered.

She looked at him hopefully. "Really? May I?"

"Sure thing," said Muscles. "C'mon, guys, let's show her the place!"

They reached the hideout after winding through two more alleys and climbing around a pile of rubble. Twilight had turned to night, and Tia stared in awe at the monstrous house of a past century, rising in dark and turreted dilapidation above the dull glow of a streetlight. The gang bunched together protectively, looked carefully around as if to make sure they were not being ambushed or watched, then quickly picked their way to a side entrance.

Dazzler removed a board across a broken door and thrust it open. Someone struck a match and lighted a kerosene lantern hidden in a corner. Tia followed them

31

inside to a large room decorated like a grotto of horror, as if somehow a frightening atmosphere would contrive to make men of steel.

White skeletons danced over black walls, grisly faces with glaring red eyes glared at them from all sides, and a hangman's noose dangled in front of a boarded-up window. A stuffed animal, too moth-eaten for identification, showed ferocious teeth from its stance beside a door, and a big dark bird with outstretched wings dangled from a string in the gloom overhead. The actual furnishings ranged from a few packing cases and boxes that served as chairs and tables, to dark, unpleasant-looking draperies that hung like shrouds between the dancing skeletons.

Tia looked slowly around. She was not greatly thrilled.

Rocky said, "Neat, hey?"

"What time do the ghosts get here?" Tia asked.

"Don't—don't say things like that," muttered Crusher, looking around nervously.

"Is this where you live?" Tia asked.

"This is where we're gonna live when we run away from home," Dazzler told her. "You can't be a tough guy and take orders from your mother or older sister."

Muscles said, "That's why we quit school. You can't be tough and educated too."

Tia opened her mouth to tell him how wrong he was, but the words never came. At that moment a hazy vision of Tony flashed through her mind. He seemed to be on his back, struggling to rise and speak.

"Tony!" she cried. "Tony!"

The Earthquakes jumped in fright and stared at her

as if she were seeing a ghost.

"Wha-what is it?" Dazzler gasped. "Wha—where?"

"I—I had contact with Tony," she said hurriedly, and put her fingers to her temples and began turning slowly around, trying to get the direction the contact had come from.

The others stared at her, mystified and uneasy. Rocky said nervously, "You—you callin' on the spirits?"

"Shhh!" she said urgently.

The contact came again, stronger and brighter this time. "Tony!" she called earnestly. "Where are you?"

Behind her the four boys, who had never experienced anything like this, stood huddled together, frightened, whispering their fears to each other and trying to deny what seemed to be going on before their eyes. To them, Tia had suddenly become creepy and weird, and the mysterious Tony, far from being another boy like themselves, was beginning to loom as an unpleasant spirit that it might be much better not to meet.

Tia did not hear their whispers. She had managed to shut them entirely out of her mind while she tried desperately to make contact with Tony.

The hazy vision of him was getting brighter.

"Tony!" she cried. "Tony!"

●   ●   ●

Tony at this moment was lying strapped to an operating table in Dr. Gannon's large and elaborately equipped laboratory, an extraordinary place that Letha Wedge had had built for him in the basement of her huge mansion on a hill above the city. After the hypodermic injection Tony had been brought there with Sickle, who, still in a zombie condition, was lying motionless on another operating table a few feet away.

Dr. Gannon, with an almost childish eagerness, had spent the day examining his rare victim. With Letha Wedge's help, he had rigged a maze of equipment to help him know and understand the possibilities of this most incredible of humans, the like of which he had never dreamed existed. Taped to Tony's forehead were a half dozen wires that led to a variety of electronic devices. His brain waves and impulses were being carefully recorded and measured. Other wires measured heart rate and blood flow, and checked for unknown waves that might contribute to his strange abilities.

Above the operating table hung a powerful light of the kind used in surgery. It was continually brightening and dimming. The doctor and his aristocratic assistant were watching it, fascinated.

"*He's* doing that?" Letha Wedge said incredulously.

"*He's* doing it," the doctor affirmed. "He's struggling for consciousness. While he struggles, he's projecting a magnetic field through his reflexes. His output is so great that my instruments aren't even capable of measuring it."

As he spoke he glanced uneasily at one of the instruments, whose needle had reached maximum. A sudden crack appeared in the glass. With a quick movement he thrust Letha Wedge aside.

The instrument exploded. Letha gave a startled scream.

"That boy's dangerous!" she exclaimed.

The doctor nodded. "He's dangerous. But once I

34

have control of his brain, he'll be dangerous only to others."

Her face hardened. "I hope you realize kidnapping is a criminal offense."

"My experiments," the doctor said aloofly, "are far more important than law."

He moved over to the other table, where the dazed Sickle was lying motionless. Turning Sickle's head to one side, he felt behind the ear and carefully removed the receptor.

With an odd, tight smile, he held the small device up and looked at it fondly for a moment. "With these receptors placed on certain important people," he said slowly, musingly, "and combined with this boy's powers, I'll become one of the most influential men in the world."

Letha Wedge's eyebrows went up. Suddenly she smiled. "You're absolutely brilliant, Professor. I've been waiting for this moment. Now we can move forward with some of my plans, too."

He gave a faint snort. "Don't bother me with your plans, Letha. They're quite empty and unimportant . . . a comment, perhaps, on you and the kind of life you've led."

Letha Wedge stiffened. Her mouth thinned and hardened. "Now just one minute, Doctor . . . Professor . . . Physicist . . . whatever you are. I built this laboratory for you at great expense, using every penny I had. We've made a lot of plans, and I won't let you upset them. I need some money—fast!"

The doctor gave her a disdainful glance, and turned away. "Letha, we're worlds apart," he said loftily. "My

35

mind is filled with large concepts: Mankind . . . the Universe. You . . . why, you merely wonder which horse is running the third race."

"Sure I gamble," Letha snapped. "But with my own money!" An edge came to her voice. "You're the worst kind of gambler: you use other people's money, then you want to keep all the winnings for yourself! But don't worry, Victor, . . . I'll be there to pick up the chips with you!"

Her temper was up and she might have said far more, but at that moment Tony moved and one of the instruments attached to him blew apart. She gasped. It was almost unbelievable, the power this boy could generate. It suddenly occurred to her that Victor was a clever fool, with no right whatever to call himself a scientist. A real scientist would be overcome with interest in the boy himself—not how he could make use of the boy's abilities for personal gain.

Then abruptly she shook her head. She couldn't afford to think this way. She needed money too badly herself. . . .

Quickly she stepped forward to help the doctor at the operating table. Tony had opened his eyes, and now he was struggling to raise his head.

"The hypo—hurry!" Dr. Gannon ordered.

Swiftly she picked up the hypodermic from the instrument tray and gave it to him. The doctor pushed Tony back on the table and thrust the needle into his arm.

● ● ●

For a few seconds after he opened his eyes, Tony fought to clear his mind and find the strength to rise.

Hazy shapes swam in his vision. . . . Was he in some kind of laboratory? Two of the shapes moved . . . a man and a woman. They seemed vaguely familiar. . . .

Then a firm hand thrust his head back to the table and he felt the bite of a needle in his arm.

Blackness overcame him again.

In the Earthquakes' hideout, Tia saw the brightness that shone in Tony's eyes, and the hazy shapes. "Tony!" she cried. "Where are you? Oh, Tony, please answer!"

Instead of an answer she felt the needle as it went into his arm, then the contact was wiped out in sudden blackness.

"It—it's all gone black!" she reported tremulously, wiping a tear from her cheek. "Now everything is completely gone."

She swallowed and sat down on one of the improvised chairs, miserable and deeply depressed. Across the room the Earthquakes, who had been keeping a safe distance from her, gave sighs of relief. The creepiness had vanished and she had become an ordinary girl again. Well, not exactly ordinary, for no other girl in the world was like Tia. But there was nothing to be afraid of now.

They came close and stood around her, and Dazzler said, "We'll be back in the morning with maps and some breakfast. When we start lookin' again we're gonna really find that Tony."

"Right," said Rocky. "And I'll bring an egg—from my own 'frigerator."

"I'll bring some day-old bread for toastin'," Crusher

promised, and Muscles said, "I'll help the guy in the grocery store in the mornin' so's he can pay me with a container of milk for you."

Dazzler wound it up by saying, "We'll give you an honest breakfast."

Tia bit her lip to hold back the tears and managed a smile for them. "Thank you," she told them earnestly. "You're good friends."

The skinny Muscles said, "That's the trouble with us. We don't wanna be good . . . we wanna be bad!"

Dazzler said, "Let's go, you guys. My Mom's gonna really yell at me."

"Yeah, we'd better go," said Crusher. "See you tomorrow, Tia."

With assurances that they would find Tony in the morning, the gang filed out, bunching close together for protection as they neared the entrance.

When she was alone, Tia sat down on one of the rough bunks that had been built along the side of the room. The dark did not frighten her, nor did the prospect of spending the night by herself in such a place as this. Her only concern was for Tony. She tried valiantly to focus her mind on him and somehow puzzle out what had happened. But she was too tired. The tears that she had been holding back for hours suddenly came in a flood.

She finally cried herself to sleep.

4

SLAVE

IT BEGAN as a perfectly beautiful day. The sun shone brightly on Letha Wedge's great house above the city, and in the trees around it the birds sang gaily as if this were a special morning to be remembered. In the spacious laboratory she had built for Dr. Gannon, everything was in order and all the equipment was humming and perking in a most satisfactory manner. Even Alfred, the laboratory goat, in his stall near the cages of guinea pigs and mice, was relishing a scrap of cardboard while he watched the goings-on in the center of the room.

On the main operating table Tony lay face down, carefully strapped in place and blindfolded. The doctor and his once-wealthy patron, attired in white smocks, were preparing to attach the receptor behind Tony's ear. Letha's nephew, Sickle, quite recovered from his unpleasant experience of the day before, stood by the instrument tray, assisting.

It was a very simple matter to attach the receptor, but the doctor, relishing the importance of it, went about it as if it were a heart transplant. Presently, with the air of a maestro whose skill is unequaled, he stepped back

39

with a little flourish of his scalpel hand, and nodded.

"Done," he said. "Turn him over and remove the blindfold."

Letha Wedge and Sickle untied the blindfold, loosened the straps, very carefully turned Tony over on his back, then tightened the straps again. The doctor drew a deep breath and picked up the remote control unit, which he had rebuilt the evening before. Ceremoniously he activated it and set all the dials.

"This is Doctor Gannon," he spoke into the microphone. "I command you to awaken!"

A little tremor went through Tony's body. Abruptly his eyes popped open. At the same time something very strange began to happen inside his head.

• • •

The sun was shining just as brightly above the slum area of the city as it was on Letha Wedge's hill, but very little of its brightness penetrated the smog. As for birdsong, not even a sparrow chirped near the hideout of the Earthquakes. But it mattered little. Tia was up, and this was a new day. Hope had returned, and she had learned long ago that if one clings to hope, then practically anything can happen.

The gang had brought her the promised breakfast, and now they were all sitting around the table, going over one of Dazzler's maps. They had marked the apparent spot where Tony had gone before he vanished, but no one was in agreement about the direction he might have taken afterward.

"If you lost 'im here," said Dazzler, putting a grimy

40

forefinger on the map, "it looks to me like he mighta gone this way." His finger traced an angular route that ended at a park.

"Aw, no . . . no! He wouldn't go that way," Crusher insisted, forgetting in his interest to talk out of the side of his mouth. "Here's what he'd do. . . ." He traced an entirely different route, to which Muscles and Rocky objected.

Tia listened quietly for a while, the conviction growing that they were all wrong. Suddenly she said, "It wasn't Tony that chose where he went. Don't you see? It—it was somebody else. If he'd had his way, he'd have come back to the taxi."

The boys stared at her. Dazzler said, "You mean . . ."

Tia swallowed. "Only two things could have happened to him. Either he was hurt and taken to a hospital. Or—or he was kidnapped."

"Kidnapped!" Dazzler exclaimed.

"Who'd kidnap 'im?" Rocky wanted to know. "Anyhow, who'd pay the ransom? You got a million dollars?"

Tia started to say that she and Tony had almost been kidnapped a year ago when they were trying to reach Witch Mountain, and that there were people in the world who probably would pay far more than a million for the use of their peculiar talents. But this would have required a long explanation, and she decided it was wiser to say nothing.

"Why don't we try—" Tia began, and abruptly stopped. For at this moment, up on Letha Wedge's hill, Dr. Gannon had activated his control unit and commanded Tony to awaken.

41

Tia suddenly sat up straight. "Tony!" she cried.

The boys around her cringed.

"There she goes again!" Rocky whispered, and began to ease away from this unexpected return to the weird. The others, equally uneasy, followed his example. Tia was left alone at the table.

Eyes closed, head raised, she said slowly, "Someone is talking to him!"

She concentrated, trying with all the power of her mind to see what Tony was seeing. There were hazy shapes, undefined . . . figures that seemed to be wearing white. . . .

• • •

In the laboratory on Letha Wedge's hill, Dr. Victor Gannon, still holding the control unit, stood by the operating table watching Tony carefully. Near him Letha was poised, eyes sharp and bright as a hawk's, a hypodermic ready in her long clawlike fingers. Sickle waited just beyond her, his receding forehead wrinkled with curiosity and expectation.

On the operating table, Tony was straining his eyes to see. He seemed to be on a table, strapped down. What sort of place was this? And those people, that man and that woman . . . who?

He had heard the voice saying, "This is Doctor Gannon. I command you to awaken!"

Now he was awake and trying hard to pull his thoughts together, but something seemed to have a grip upon them. Next he made an attempt to move, and could not. He might have been paralyzed. In his inner mind he heard Tia's distant, urgent call, "Tony!" and he tried with all his might to answer, but he seemed to have lost the power to do so.

Angrily, furiously, desperately, he fought to break away from the grip that held his mind. While he fought, he heard the voice of Dr. Gannon saying, "You will now function exclusively under control. You will no longer think independently. All thinking and reasoning will be done by the voice that commands you. Do you understand?"

"Yes," he heard himself reply, in a curiously flat tone that did not sound like himself. His fury rose and he tried to shout a denial at this man who wanted to control him and turn him into a slave. But he was unable to make a sound. His tongue belonged to Dr. Gannon.

But I don't belong to you! he told himself, and gave a desperate mental jerk that tore the *I* part of him free, so that he seemed to fall back within his own skull, a small frightened, confused being who was confined in the space behind his eyes, but was somehow free to think his own thoughts. This being that was his inner self, and *himself* alone, had nothing to do with the captive outer self—the brain and body that had been stolen from him and over which he no longer had the slightest control.

"What is your name?" Dr. Gannon was demanding.

"Tony," he heard himself say, though he fought for silence.

"Where are you from, Tony?"

"Witch Mountain."

"Must be a hick town," said another man—a young man with a receding brow he could see vaguely beyond

43

the doctor. Was that the man he'd saved from falling?

"How," the doctor asked slowly, "did you suspend Mr. Sickle in midair?"

"By energizing matter," he heard his voice say woodenly—and raged inwardly because he hadn't let the arrogant and snaky Mr. Sickle fall to his death. But no, he couldn't have done that. No one could who had made the long journey from the dying planet of the two suns to this strange and greedy world. Life was too precious. You did all you could to save it.

Dr. Gannon, with something like amazement in his voice, was now saying, "Do you mean to tell me that you can control molecular flow?"

"Yes, sir."

"How did you learn to do this?"

"I was born with the ability."

Dr. Gannon grunted and stood thoughtfully for a moment. Abruptly he said, "I wish to see a demonstration of molecular flow. You are strapped to the table. I command you to unbuckle yourself!"

Tony's inner self was aware that his captive self raised his head, studied the straps that held him to the table, and then energized them.

While the straps were unbuckling themselves, his eyes were able to take in more of the room, and he saw the woman on the other side of the doctor. She was the one who had talked so sweetly to him and held his attention while the doctor had plunged the hypodermic needle into his back. The rage he had felt earlier rose again. *Buzzards!* he screamed silently from the prison of his skull. *Buzzards! Rotten, dirty buzzards!*

The doctor and his two assistants stood watching in

44

amazement while the straps, as if manipulated by invisible hands, finished unbuckling themselves and hung straight down from the table. Tony, zombielike, sat up stiffly while his inner self continued to rage.

"Excellent! Excellent!" Dr. Gannon purred, as if highly pleased with what the future held. "You have fantastic possibilities. I think it's time to take you out on a shakedown cruise . . . to find out what you can really do."

Tony's head turned automatically, watching him, and for the first time he was able to view a large portion of the laboratory. To his inner eye it was a hazy view, but it occurred to him that Tia might be able to see it also if she was still trying to contact him. His rage subsided as he tried to take in as much of his surroundings as possible.

• • •

Tia, at that moment, caught a quick, hazy view of what Tony was seeing, but the mental picture faded almost as quickly as it came. Even so, her unusually retentive memory clung to the vision.

Eyes closed, she tried to tell the others what she had seen. "Tony . . . he's in some kind of room with . . . white tables and things . . . like a hospital. . . . There are machines and instruments and . . . and things . . ."

"Hey, that's easy!" Dazzler exclaimed. "All we gotta do is check the hospitals."

"Right!" said Crusher, remembering now to speak out of the side of his mouth. "We'll check 'em while we're goin' around lookin' for a fight."

45

Muscles said, "C'mon, you guys! Let's get goin'!"

They grabbed Tia's hands and headed quickly for the door.

• • •

In the laboratory, Tony was sitting up stiffly on the operating table, awaiting further instructions. His inner self was aware that Letha Wedge was watching him carefully, the hypodermic needle ever ready in her hand. Sickle was also watching him, his heavy eyebrows raised in an attitude somewhere between astonishment and absolute disbelief. Only Dr. Gannon seemed thoroughly inspired.

"It's hard to believe!" the doctor exclaimed happily. "A power has come into our hands centuries ahead of its time. We must use it wisely."

"What will we have him do?" Letha Wedge asked, her voice rising. "Have him go around making people's belts open?"

"The possibilities are unlimited," the doctor said expansively.

Sickle's mouth twitched. "Come on, now. It's just some kind of a gimmick, that's all."

Dr. Gannon turned and looked him over coldly, then smiled chillingly and said to Tony, "Tony, Mr. Sickle, whose life you saved, still doesn't believe in you. He's tired, physically and mentally. He should rest. Help him to sleep, Tony. . . . Give him a snootful of ether."

The doctor indicated an anesthetic stand to the right of the table, and gave a little nod.

46

The inner Tony watched, suddenly fascinated, while his other self activated the stand. The rubber mask, attached to it by a hose, rose cobralike and moved toward Sickle's face.

Sickle yelped and backed fearfully away. "Hey, wait a minute . . . wait!" He tried to wave the thing off, and said hoarsely, "Go away! Go away!"

Instead, Sickle was forced to flee and the stand pursued him. It pursued him relentlessly like a live thing, the cobralike mask weaving in front of it, threatening at any moment to strike. Finally it did strike. It backed Sickle into a corner against a piece of equipment, the mask slapped itself over his face, and the quivering Sickle, powerless to remove it, suddenly crumpled.

The inner Tony heard Dr. Gannon chuckle, highly pleased. Then Letha Wedge said, "I can see how the boy would be a big hit at a scientific convention, but the bottom line is: How do we make money with him?"

"Oh, we'll make money with him," the doctor assured her. "Come, Tony. We'll all go down into the cellar and show her a little industrial application."

Tony was directed across the laboratory and down a flight of steps to another level where a number of wine casks had been left in the middle of the floor.

The doctor pointed, and said, "Tony, stack the wine casks neatly over yonder."

The casks were activated, and then levitated to the chosen spot and stacked neatly in a pyramid. While it was being done, the inner Tony did his best to drop one of the casks on Dr. Gannon's head, but he was powerless to do a thing. The outer Tony followed the orders exactly.

"Now, Tony," the doctor said, "serve us two glasses of burgundy."

The glasses were levitated from a table to a wine cask. A spigot was opened, the glasses were filled, then they were levitated into Letha's and the doctor's hands.

The doctor smiled and raised his glass. "To molecular mobilization!" he said grandly.

Letha Wedge, who obviously had been greatly impressed by all these demonstrations, gave a thin, calculating smile and raised her glass.

"To molecular capitalization!" she said determinedly.

While the captive Tony stood passively by, the inner Tony looked on and silently raged.

5

GOLD RUSH

IT HAD BEEN a very discouraging day, but Tia was not yet ready to give up. While the weary Earthquakes straggled behind her, watching, she moved slowly down the street, eyes closed, fingers touching her temples, while she tried again and again to contact Tony.

Rocky, suddenly wondering about the continual movement of her fingers to her head, looked at Crusher and said, "She's been doin' that for hours. Y'think she's okay?"

"Maybe she's got a headache," Crusher offered. "I sorta got one myself. It's been a no-good day."

Dazzler said, "Tia? Y'gettin' any clues?"

Tia opened her eyes and gave a dispirited shake of her head. "No," she murmured. "Nothing at all. It's so strange. . . ."

"I can't figure it," said Muscles. "We've been to every hospital, and he's not in any of them."

Tia shook her head. "It's like his mind is a blank."

"He must be conked out," muttered Crusher out of the side of his mouth.

Tia was obviously upset by Crusher's remark. The

49

others gave him a push, and Dazzler said, "Don't listen to him, Tia."

Rocky took Tia's hand. "Tomorrow, we're gonna find Tony for sure."

"Right," said Muscles, taking Tia's other hand. "Tomorrow we'll turn this town upside down."

The hideout was just ahead. In the evening light the hideous old structure looked anything but inviting, but Tia glimpsed it with relief. It had been, as Crusher had said, a no-good day.

But tomorrow . . .

● ● ●

As darkness settled over the city, Letha Wedge went to the desk in her study. Opening a bottom drawer, she took out a group of plans and photographs she had hidden there and was going over them carefully when she heard the door behind her open. She looked up sharply and started to conceal the plans, then she saw that the intruder was her nephew, Sickle.

"Got the horses picked for tomorrow?" Sickle asked, giving her a conspiratorial grin.

"I'm thinking . . . planning . . ."

"Good!" He grinned again. "We need a couple of winners. We owe every bookie in town."

"We have a winner," she told him. "A big winner!"

He raised his eyebrows. "The daily double?"

"My dear nephew," she began patiently, "think of us in a different place . . . such as . . . Las Vegas . . . with Tony. Imagine us at the roulette table: Tony makes our

50

number win each time. Then we move to the crap table and throw the dice."

"Seven or eleven every time, right?"

She nodded. "And imagine a day at the races with Tony . . ."

"All the long shots come in, eh?"

"You do have an imagination after all," she replied. "Yes, the possibilities with Tony are unlimited. For example, . . . today he stacked the wine casks just by looking at them. If he can stack them, . . . he can unstack them."

She gave him a twisted little smile and handed him a photograph of a pyramid of gold.

"What's this?" Sickle muttered. "Gold? Yeah, gold!"

"Three million dollars' worth," she told him. "Enough to pay back our creditors and bookies, plus some pocket money for us. The gold is on display at the museum, protected by an impenetrable security system. Just sitting there—waiting for us to penetrate it."

"Us?" said her nephew. "You mean Gannon said it's okay to use the control and Tony?"

She sniffed. "Doctor Professor Gannon is extremely busy being a genius. I own half the invention and half of Tony. That means I own half the profits. So far, the only return on my investment has been half of zero."

Sickle growled, "All I'm getting is a bald spot where he keeps attaching that thing."

"Then," said Letha, holding up the photograph of the gold, "isn't it time to get—something?"

"Yeah, but what about security? We'd need an army to pull it off."

Letha smiled again. "We'll have an army with us—Tony."

Sickle snapped his fingers and grinned. "Aunt Letha, you're too much!"

• • •

In the Earthquakes' hideout down in the darkness of the city, Tia finally gave up trying to sleep. While her eyes watched the skeletons on the wall—they seemed to dance in the flickering light of the lantern—her mind grappled with the problem of what could have happened to Tony.

They had checked the hospitals, so it was very unlikely that he had been in an accident. That left kidnapping.

But who could have kidnapped Tony? And why?

Tony had been gone only a few minutes when it had happened. Furthermore, it had happened in a strange place, evidently on the spur of the moment, so it must have been done by a complete stranger. But what would prompt a stranger, who didn't know anything about Tony, to kidnap him?

Could the falling body have had anything to do with it? Had the stranger watched Tony degravitate, or possibly energize, the person who was falling? That must be it. And a hypodermic must have been used to make Tony unconscious—for she had felt the jab of it herself at the time she had lost contact with him.

And where was Tony now? Locked away in some horrible private laboratory where she might never be able to find him?

The thought brought her to tears and made her more miserable than ever.

Suddenly she sat up, and with all the power she possessed, she sent forth another call to him: "Tony . . . Tony . . . Tony . . . Can you hear me? Why can't I get through to you? Tony . . ."

The captive Tony, asleep on a cot in a basement room in Letha Wedge's great house on a hill, stirred uneasily at the call but did not waken. He could not waken so long as the control unit, on a nearby table, had the red light turned on. But the inner Tony heard and tried frantically to call back. Again and again he tried, even though he well knew he did not have the power to send it beyond the skull that imprisoned him.

Finally, when he could no longer hear Tia, he gave up the attempt to answer and began wondering what tomorrow had in store for him. From what he had overheard—and even Dr. Gannon had failed to discover there was a part of him capable of overhearing a great deal, even through closed doors—the members of this scheming household were far from agreement on anything. And Letha Wedge and her nephew had plans of their own. Plans, something told him, that would mean trouble for everyone. . . .

• • •

While the captive Tony slept on into the morning, the inner Tony listened to the sounds of activity through the house—people getting up, having breakfast, preparing to go about their business for the day. Presently, in the driveway somewhere beyond the window of the

53

room where he lay, he heard Letha Wedge and Sickle talking to Dr. Gannon, then the sound of a car door being closed.

He heard the doctor say, "I'll pick up the new transistors, make a few stops, and be back later on. By noon, I hope."

"Take your time, Victor," Letha Wedge told him. "Everything will be under control."

Sure, Tony thought. You'll have *me* under control. He didn't like the idea one bit, but there was nothing whatever he could do about it. He heard the doctor start the motor and then the soft purr of the car moving down the driveway.

Almost immediately Sickle whispered, "Let's go!"

Seconds later Tony heard Sickle and Letha come into his room. He could not see them, for his eyes were closed, but evidently Letha picked up the control unit, because Sickle muttered, "You sure you know how to use it?"

"Of course I'm sure," Letha replied tartly. "I'm very good with mechanical things."

There were buttons on the control unit that had to be pressed a certain way. Apparently she did it right, for all at once she ordered, "Tony! This is Letha Wedge commanding you to open your eyes."

His eyes popped open, and he saw the two of them looking at him intently, anxiously. He got up slowly and stood before them, a little stiffly, like a robot awaiting orders from a master.

"Okay, Tony," Letha said. "We're going to the museum today—for education and profit. Follow me."

He followed her into the garage, and they got into

54

Sickle's car. Sickle drove them into the city and parked next to the museum.

They got out, and Letha, giving her nephew an encouraging pat on the shoulder, said quietly, "You'll stay here and have the trunk open."

"You sure you won't need me inside, Aunt Letha?"

She gave a low chuckle. "The molecules will be doing all the work. Tony and I will just stand there and control it all. No one will know we're involved. Soon as your trunk is loaded . . . get going. Don't worry about us. See you later. . . ." Then she said into the control, "Okay, Tony, . . . let's do a little sight-seeing."

While Sickle turned to open the trunk of his car, Tony went up the steps with her and entered the museum.

The theme of the exhibit was the Gold Rush. At another time the inner Tony might have enjoyed it, for the displays showed everything from the panning and early production of gold to the processing and coining of it, along with the various vehicles and machinery associated with it. But he had no eyes for what was shown, for every step he took with Letha Wedge only added to his uneasiness.

Finally they reached the main part of the exhibit that was attracting everyone. In a circular showcase, enclosed in a special plastic shield, lay a gleaming pyramid of gold bars. The place was surrounded by security guards who were carefully scrutinizing the tourists who filed past.

As Tony stared at the incredible pyramid of gold, Tia, who was just leaving the hideout with the Earthquakes, stopped short.

"Gold!" she gasped. "I see gold!"

"Where?" said Dazzler, as the others looked eagerly around. "I don't see none."

"I—I don't know where it is," Tia said. "But it has something to do with Tony . . ."

At the exhibit, Tony found himself drawn away from the pyramid of gold and his attention directed to an old stagecoach.

"Tony," Letha Wedge said into the control unit, "we're about to create a diversion. Look at that stagecoach. I command you to make it roll around the room!"

Knowing what was coming, the inner Tony winced and wished he could be anywhere but here. Then he raged because he was powerless to stop the captive Tony from doing what was ordered.

Slowly, creaking loudly, the stagecoach began to roll across the room. People scurried out of its way and turned to gape at it in disbelief. Someone shouted and pointed, and suddenly everyone was staring at it as it began to circle the gold display.

At that moment Tia, going up the street with the Earthquakes, stopped short again.

"I see a stagecoach!" she exclaimed. "It's moving!"

Rocky looked quickly around and shook his head. "I don't see nothin' like that."

Muscles said, "She must be tuned in on a Western."

Over at the museum the startled security guards stared openmouthed at the circling stagecoach, but refused to leave their posts at the gold display. Letha Wedge eyed them with momentary dismay, then spun Tony around to face a row of ore carts in a display of a tunnel entrance. The last cart had the dummy of a miner leaning against it in a pushing position.

"Quick, Tony," she ordered, "make the ore carts chase the security guards!"

To the inner Tony, watching the ore carts begin to roll, scattering the security guards and everyone in their path, this was the beginning of complete pandemonium and madness. For in the next breath Letha Wedge was commanding that all the dummies and everything movable in the place be activated.

This shocked the inner Tony, for there were dummies everywhere in the exhibit: gold panners, old-time cowboys, frontier settlers, and even a cigar-store Indian with a raised tomahawk. One by one they came to life and began moving about, adding to the growing confusion. In seconds the place was in an uproar. The inner Tony trembled, for Letha Wedge had only begun to give orders, and he dreaded to think what the next few minutes would be like.

With an effort he managed to turn his inner vision away from the increasingly mad scene that the captive Tony was being forced to create and tried to imagine himself back at Witch Mountain. Instead he received a series of sudden flashes, none of them very clear, that showed Tia first, and then Dr. Gannon.

Tia seemed to be heading for the museum with a gang of boys, which made no sense whatever. On the other hand, a very angry Dr. Gannon, who had come home early, was also headed for the museum. This meant trouble piled upon trouble.

6

UTTER MADNESS

FOR THE THIRD TIME since leaving the hideout
with the Earthquakes to search for Tony, Tia stopped
abruptly. Her fingers went to her forehead as she caught
glimpses of objects in her mind.

"I'm seeing . . . old things," she said, eyes closed.
"Clothing . . . long dresses . . . bonnets . . . furniture . . ."

Dazzler snapped his fingers. "That Tony, he's at the
Salvation Army!"

"Aw," said Crusher, "they don't got stagecoaches at
the Salvation Army."

"And they don't got gold neither," Rocky added.

"Wait a minute . . . wait a minute!" said Dazzler.
"That lousy school we go to. . . . We had one of them
nothin' class trips to the museum—"

"I remember that trip," Muscles told him. "I played
hooky from it."

"They got a big pile of gold there—and a stagecoach!" Dazzler exclaimed. "They hadda chase me outa
it!"

58

Tia was suddenly excited. "We've got to go there!" she cried.

"Then let's go!" said Dazzler. "Follow me!" He started off at a run, with Tia and the others close behind.

"Aaaah . . . it's too edjacational," Rocky complained, but he hurried along after the rest.

• • •

Tia and the Earthquakes had just started for the museum when Dr. Gannon, having finished his business earlier than expected, arrived back at Letha Wedge's house on the hill. No one answered his call when he entered, and there was still no answer when he reached the laboratory. With rising uneasiness he rushed to Tony's room, saw the empty cot, and discovered that the control unit was missing from the table. Furious now, he ran back into the laboratory, knocking instruments and parts to the floor as he searched wildly for the control unit. Not finding it, he tore into Letha's study. Almost immediately he noticed the photograph on her desk—a picture of the gold bars. It told him all he needed to know.

"The museum!" he gasped. "The fool! The utter fool!"

Shaking with rage and sudden anxiety—for Letha could ruin all their plans—he raced outside and got into his car.

Long before Dr. Gannon came in sight of the place, the museum was in an uproar. Tourists, attendants, and guards were running around frantically trying to stop the wildly moving ore carts and stagecoach, and succeeding only in colliding with each other or in being knocked aside by the moving dummies. These, in their costumes, seemed like a group of people of another era who had invaded the museum and were trying to take it over. The miner pushing an ore cart was grimly charging a guard with it, while the cigar-store Indian, with raised tomahawk, was striking terror at every turn.

Letha Wedge, as if not satisfied with the present havoc, drew Tony's attention to a large glass window high on the wall above the display of gold. The security controller, his mouth hanging open in disbelief, was standing before the glass, staring down at the pandemonium. As Letha Wedge pointed to him, he whirled, leaped to the banks of security equipment behind him, and grasped a knob.

"Quick, Tony!" Letha ordered. "Make the security system break down!"

The inner Tony winced as the captive Tony carried out the order. Abruptly the banks of security equipment began going to pieces and falling apart. They collapsed on the floor in a pile of junk. The incredulous controller was left with a knob in his hand.

Next Letha pointed to the assay furnace where ore was tested. "Ignite it!" she said. "Hurry!"

Oh, no! No! the inner Tony cried soundlessly. *Haven't you done enough?* But the cry went unheard, for already the captive Tony obligingly had ignited the furnace and it was flaring high. Three security guards, momentarily escaping from the charging ore trucks, shouted in alarm and made feeble attempts to put out the flame.

The museum by now had become a madhouse.

Letha Wedge clutched Tony's arm and indicated the gleaming pyramid of metal behind the plastic shield.

"The gold!" she cried, her voice quavering with excitement. "The gold! This is our chance to get it out! Tony, make a hole in the plastic so the bars can come through. It doesn't have to be neat."

You can't do it! the inner Tony said prayerfully, as the captive Tony concentrated on the plastic. *You're not a human ray gun! No one's ever taught you*—Then his plea turned into a silent groan as a section of the plastic began to bend and bubble. Slowly the section dissolved, leaving a large hole.

"Tony, levitate the gold bars!" Letha Wedge ordered excitedly. "Fly them through the air, out the front door, and deliver them to Mr. Sickle at the car! Now!"

The inner Tony cringed and tried not to watch as the pyramid of gold became energized. Suddenly the top bar rose, moved through the air and out of the hole, and across the room over the heads of the people toward the front door. A second gold bar rose and followed the first. A third bar and then a fourth followed the others, and more came on from behind. Evenly spaced a few yards apart, they zoomed over the careening stagecoach and flew out of the door, which automatically swung open as they approached.

A happily amazed Letha Wedge hugged herself and cried gaily, "Las Vegas, here we come!"

Then her gaiety changed to nervousness as she stood

61

watching the slow movement of the bars through the door. Suddenly realizing how long it would take to move all the gold a bar at a time, her hands clenched and she ordered, "Faster, Tony! Faster! Get the rest of it out there together!"

The remainder of the gold rose as a mass into the air, smashed a larger hole through the plastic shield, and sailed away over the heads of the shouting guards and the gaping and bewildered onlookers. It followed the last bar through the open door and vanished outside. . . .

• • •

Tia and the Earthquakes were rounding the corner near the museum when the gleaming line of gold bars came through the door. They saw it dip down over the flight of steps to the street and snake away to the spot where Sickle's car was parked. At the sight of it they stopped abruptly and stared at it incredulously, not immediately sure what it was or what was happening.

They made out Sickle in the distance attempting to catch the bars and put them in the trunk of his car. But they were coming too fast and evidently the weight of them was more than he could handle, for he kept staggering about and dropping them while trying to dodge others that hit him. Then, as they rained upon him, he lost his balance and fell against the car, accidentally slamming the trunk closed without having placed a single bar inside.

Now it almost seemed that he was being attacked by the bars. They pelted him and slammed upon the car, denting the sides and the trunk. One bar smashed the rear window, and continued all the way through and crashed out the windshield, falling on the hood and denting it badly.

Suddenly Tia realized what was going on. "That—that's gold!" she cried. "And it has to be Tony who's making it fly out like that. He's inside!"

"C'mon!" said Dazzler. "I sure wanna see this Tony!"

They raced along the street and dashed up the flight of steps to the museum. Inside they stopped short, looking around incredulously.

The pandemonium was now at its height. Men were shouting and women were screaming. The stagecoach and the ore cars and everything that could move were racing madly about without rhyme or reason. Some attendants had managed to get aboard the stagecoach and were trying in vain to stop it by straining on the brakes. Other people were throwing benches and chairs in the path of the racing ore cars, while groups of guards —those who had not been laid low by previous violence —were fighting the costumed dummies to prevent them from running amok with shotgun, pickax, or tomahawk, as they seemed bent upon doing.

It might have been a scene from a nightmare.

The four Earthquakes could only stare at it with glazed eyes, for once utterly speechless. But Tia, immediately upon entering, knew exactly what had happened, and what to do about it.

She closed her eyes and clenched her slender hands tightly.

Alarms began to ring for the first time. The stagecoach coasted to a stop, the badly jolted men on it still straining at the brake. Tia concentrated harder. Life went out of the gyrating costumed figures and they became motionless dummies again. The rattling ore carts stopped and from the last one crawled an angry and disheveled guard who shook his fist at the lifeless dummy of a miner that had been pushing it. Tia made a last desperate effort. The fire died in the assay furnace, and all around it the mad confusion began to quiet.

People shook their heads, looked at each other, and gasped, "What in the world happened?"

The first to ask that question was a suddenly shaken Letha Wedge. She looked quickly at Tony, and demanded, "What happened?"

In his peculiarly wooden voice the captive Tony said, "The molecular flow has been reversed."

Letha seemed shocked. "D-did you do it?"

"No."

"Then—then who did?"

"It would have to be one of my people."

The shock in Letha's face was swiftly changing to fright. "You—you mean there are more like you?"

"Yes."

Letha swallowed, then said grimly, "Let's get out of here!"

She seized Tony's arm and rushed toward the door.

Tia, standing with the Earthquakes just to the right of the entrance, happened to turn her head and see Tony and Letha Wedge hurrying toward the exit door on the left.

"There he is!" she cried and ran to intercept Tony before the rapacious-looking woman with him could draw him outside. "Tony! Tony!"

64

Without stopping, Tony and Letha turned their heads, and Letha asked quickly, "Who's that?"

"My sister," the captive Tony answered woodenly, "my sister, Tia." At the same time the inner Tony cried out joyfully, *Tia! Tia! I'm so glad you're here! This woman has me in her control. Take me away from her!*

Tia could not hear the silent plea, but she felt something without quite knowing what it was. Before she could decide what to do, Letha snapped, "This is no time for family reunions!" and forcibly herded Tony out of the door.

People were already crowding to the exit, and Tia suddenly found her way blocked by a succession of broad backs she could see neither over nor around.

"Tony!" she shrilled. "Tony! Tony!"

Desperately she began fighting her way through the door, yet even with the Earthquakes helping it was some time before she gained the steps outside. Tony and the woman who had him by the arm had already reached the street and were racing toward the car she had seen earlier being battered by the gold bars.

"Hurry!" she cried to the Earthquakes. "We've got to catch them! Something's wrong! That woman . . ."

• • •

Sickle's car had been thoroughly crushed and ruined by the rain of gold bars, and Sickle himself, who had not been nimble enough to dodge all the gold that came his way, was on the ground struggling to get up. The final flight of bars was on top of the wrecked car, neatly stacked in a pyramid.

At the sight of the scattered gold and the wreck, Letha Wedge stopped as if she had been shot. Her mouth came open and she could only stare incredulously at this undreamed-of ruination of her plans. Her hands trembled and she struggled to speak, but before words could come she was further shaken by the screech of a car that came skidding to a stop beyond the wreck.

Dr. Gannon leaped out and ran around to the front of his car, then stiffened with an oath and stared grimly at the gold and the wreckage.

Letha was suddenly brought to her senses by the sound of Tia calling frantically to Tony. With a quick glance over her shoulder that took in Tia as well as the questionable gang with her, she gave Tony's arm a jerk and ran toward the doctor's car.

Looking up and seeing her, Dr. Gannon twisted his mouth wrathfully. "You fool!" he snapped. "How could you do this?"

"Not now!" Letha said hoarsely. "Let's go! Tony's sister's right behind us!"

She ran to the rear door of his car, jerked it open, and hustled Tony and the doctor inside. Sickle, on his feet now, was staggering toward the car. She thrust him into the driver's seat and got in beside him. "If you're able to drive," she said urgently, "get going! Hurry!"

Sickle bent over the wheel, mouth thinning. He gunned the motor, which was still running, and they pulled away from the museum with tires screaming.

No one thought to look back, so no one saw Tia run to the edge of the sidewalk and concentrate upon them. But all at once the motor began to sputter. The car

66

slowed, the motor suddenly died, and they coasted to a stop.

"What the devil's the matter?" the doctor demanded.

"I—I don't know!" Sickle told him. "I keep this car runnin' perfect!"

"It has to be Tony's sister!" Letha cried. "She did it! She's as weird as he is!"

Dr. Gannon jerked around and stared out of the rear window. His jaws knotted. He turned back and said harshly, "Tony, I command you to make the motor of this car run perfectly and continuously, and without any interference from your sister!"

The inner Tony begged, *No! No! Leave the motor alone! This is our chance to get away!* The captive Tony hesitated, as if he was faintly aware that something was not as it should be. But the command won out. Slowly he energized the motor. It sputtered back to life, then roared with power. The car shot forward, nearly giving the passengers whiplash.

Dr. Gannon looked through the rear window again. He smiled grimly at the sight of the small girl standing at the edge of the street behind him, hands tightly clenched. Then the smile faded as he turned away.

7

CHASE

TIA had run into the street, trying with all her power to stop again the car that was taking Tony away. It had been easy the first time, and she had managed it without effort. But now it was impossible to do a thing.

"I can't stop them!" she wailed. "Tony must have taken over. I—I can't understand . . ."

The Earthquakes had crowded around her, watching the car with Tony in it recede in the distance. No one noticed the Board of Education minibus pass them on the opposite side of the street, but the driver saw them. He raced to the corner, made a quick turn and raced back, and came to a screeching stop just behind Tia and the Earthquakes.

The Earthquakes jumped with fright and spun around. Before anyone could quite comprehend what was happening, the burly little driver was out of the bus in a flash and had collared Crusher and Muscles.

"Gotcha!" he snapped, a look of grim delight on his round bulldoggish face. "I've been dreaming of this moment!"

Tia recognized the truant officer, Mr. Yokomoto, but

for seconds, with her anguished attention on the car taking Tony away, she was only partially aware that the Earthquakes were in trouble.

Crusher was yelling, "Leggo! Ouch! Help! I don't wanna go to school!" And skinny Muscles was squealing and making desperate but utterly useless attempts to break the iron grip that held him.

Then a frightened and confused Dazzler suddenly caught Tia's arm and begged, "C-can't you *do* something?"

Tia turned around and faced Mr. Yokomoto, who in turn gave her the sort of pleased look that a hungry wolverine might bestow upon an extra rabbit.

"Okay, miss," he bit out. "Why aren't *you* in school?"

Tia glanced at the minibus, and her eyes turned quickly to the car with Tony in it, which was almost out of sight in the distance. Then she looked again at the minibus.

Suddenly she nodded as if coming to a decision, and said quickly, "Okay. Everybody into the bus! Hurry!"

The Earthquakes groaned and Rocky burst out, "You crazy?" Dazzler begged, "D-don't do this to us, Tia!"

Tia ignored them and said to Mr. Yokomoto, "Sir, do you see that big dark car way up the street? It's just now stopping at the red light."

The truant officer looked, and Tia said, "Well, my brother is in it, and he ought to be in school too. We should catch up with him."

"Another truant, eh?" The burly little officer grinned. "What a load this'll be!"

Tia exchanged hurried glances with the boys and gave a little jerk of her head. The Earthquakes got the idea and scrambled aboard.

Mr. Yokomoto followed quickly, the smug grin still on his face. Before he could settle in his seat Tia energized the motor and the gearshift, and the minibus jumped forward as if it had been given a violent push.

"Hey, wait a minute!" the officer cried, grabbing desperately at the wheel.

"We can't let my brother get away," Tia reminded him, and energized the accelerator pedal.

With a sudden wild roar and the smell of burning rubber, the minibus was catapulted down the street. It shot through an intersection where a green light mysteriously flashed on when it should have stayed red. Then it whipped around a corner on one wheel without changing speed or angle and tore down another street as if pursued by demons. Second by second it crept closer to the black car ahead.

Though Tia was in complete control, this did nothing to ease the fears of the Earthquakes who cowered in the seats behind her. Once Mr. Yokomoto, frightened out of his wits by a machine that seemed to have gone quite mad, tried to turn off the motor and apply the brakes. But nothing worked as it should, and the minibus raced on. Mr. Yokomoto clung to the wheel, too busy to think, grimly fighting his way through traffic as if every second might be his last. More than once, when a collision seemed impossible to avoid, the wheel spun through his hands in spite of his grip upon it, and the minibus leaped to safety without even a scratch in its paint.

70

Not until the black car was close enough for her to see clearly Tony in the backseat did Tia feel her first tremor of uneasiness. Though she had no idea what means had been used to change Tony into the stranger he had become, it was obvious that he was completely in the power of the people with him. He had to do exactly what they told him.

As she thought ahead, trying to guess what moves they might possibly make to prevent her from overtaking them, she realized with a sudden twinge of fear that they might order Tony to wreck the minibus. He could do it so very easily, and almost in a flash, unless she was extremely watchful.

Suddenly she saw Tony's captor glare back at her through the rear window of his car, then speak quickly to Tony.

Here it comes! she thought.

Ahead of the black car she made out a cement truck parked on the right. Tia clenched her lip and quickly energized the seat belts. They snaked forth and buckled themselves around the occupants of the minibus. The cement truck shot out from its parking spot just as the black car passed it.

The Earthquakes gasped, and Rocky yelled, "Look out!"

Mr. Yokomoto froze at the wheel, eyes popping at the sight of inescapable doom. Tia had already energized the wheel, and now she made it spin through his hands.

The minibus swerved hard and might have made it if the street had been wider with less traffic on it. But there was a sudden bang and an ugly tearing sound as the rear corner hit the end of the truck, and a section of the minibus was ripped open like a tin can. Part of it hung down behind and could be heard dragging on the street.

Mr. Yokomoto risked a backward glance and gave a horrified yelp. "City property!" he squealed, his voice rising as he grasped the enormity of what he had done. "I've damaged city property!"

Tia bit her lip, but she had no time for him. She righted the skidding minibus, sent it roaring after the black car, and tried to keep her mind alert to what the stranger who was Tony might do next.

The moment she saw the big city bus approaching on the other side of the street, she had a feeling Tony would attempt to do something with it. He did, for abruptly the big bus veered into their path. It swung broadside, blocking the entire street.

Tia gave a little prayer that she would have power enough, then she swung the minibus to the rear of the city bus and concentrated upon it.

The rear end of the city bus rose jerkily into the air like an uncertain drawbridge, allowing the minibus to shoot under it. It almost got through, but not quite. There were squeals and cries of terror as something on the underside of the larger bus caught the roof of the minibus and peeled it back as if it were a tin of sardines. The little bus sped on without diminishing speed, its roof hanging down and scraping on the paving behind with a loud and horrible rasping sound that put everyone's teeth on edge.

"I don't believe this!" Mr. Yokomoto quavered. "It cannot happen. And it is city property! What am I going to do?" Then he pleaded, "Maybe we—we'd better let that—that truant get away!"

The terrified Earthquakes were huddled together behind Tia, beyond speech. But a moment later they were incoherently crying out and pointing as a new obstruction was forced across their path. This time it was a tandem trailer.

Tia, hands clenched, concentrated on the trailer coupling. It opened, and the vehicles pulled apart just in time for the minibus to squeeze through. But it was too tight a squeeze, for the sides were pulled back, leaving the occupants exposed. Tia was on the point of tears by now. Dismally she wondered how much more she and the poor minibus could take.

Then she shook her head and managed to pull herself together, preparing for the next ordeal that she knew was bound to come—unless, of course, she could reach the black car and somehow get Tony away from the people who had kidnapped him. Just how she would manage this she wasn't quite sure, but with the Earthquakes and Mr. Yokomoto helping, it shouldn't be too hard. Though the bulldoggish little truant officer wasn't very big, she had a feeling he knew all sorts of tricks that would make him more than the equal of the men in the car ahead.

The next obstacle almost caught her unawares. She didn't notice the freight car parked on a siding until the black car had crossed the railroad track. Before she reached the track, the freight car rolled swiftly out from the siding and blocked the roadway.

It was almost too late to swerve, and Tia had only a

brief second to decide that levitation was probably their best chance. The decision wouldn't have bothered any of the oldsters at Witch Mountain. They were adept at it and with the greatest of ease they could move tons at a time. But the heaviest thing Tia had ever lifted alone was the rear end of the city bus somewhere behind them, and she had really flunked that because she hadn't lifted it high enough.

But there wasn't time to worry about it. Mr. Yokomoto was screaming, "I can't control it! Look out!" And Dazzler and the others were whimpering and giving gasps of horror.

Tia hardly heard them. Instantly she put all she had into concentrating *up*—and up they went, sailing over the freight car at breakneck speed, as neat as you please, and then down they came to a perfect four-point landing, easily and without a bounce or a jolt and with speed undiminished.

I did it! she thought, pleased with her achievement, though there was no one in a condition to congratulate her. Mr. Yokomoto and the Earthquakes were too limp from shock, and the man in the car ahead could only give her an astonished glare, obviously and definitely wishing she was dead.

Something about the man gave her a chill that wouldn't go away. He's the one I've got to watch, she told herself. The woman and the driver are scheming and greedy, but they are not really tough or smart. That's the smart one, and he's tough. He'll kill me if he gets a chance, because I'm upsetting his plans.

The chill in her deepened into fear, and she watched

the man carefully, trying to pick up his thoughts and guess what his next move would be. The minibus, in spite of its nearly wrecked condition, was creeping closer and closer. The man spoke quickly to the driver. Abruptly the black car skidded around the next corner and streaked away, motor roaring, on a new course.

Tia's final sight of the man was just before the black car vanished around the corner. He was talking rapidly to Tony and pointing to something ahead.

Seconds later the minibus skidded around the same corner. There was an instant when Tia glimpsed a tall building ahead whose glass sides sharply reflected the sun. But it was the briefest of glimpses. Almost immediately she was struck by a blinding light that made it impossible to see anything.

Tony must have been ordered to magnify the sun's reflection on the building. Nothing else could have caused such instant brilliance. Desperately she tried to stop it. She might have succeeded if she had been able to locate the exact spot the brilliance came from, but this was impossible. She was temporarily blinded and could see nothing but glaring whiteness.

Mr. Yokomoto cried, "I can't see!"

Rocky and the others yelled, "Turn it off! Turn it off!"

She couldn't turn off the glare. Suddenly she realized she had better stop the speeding minibus before something terrible happened. Instantly she cut the motor and energized the brakes. The action came a moment too late. The minibus careened into a solid structure on the left, glanced off, and sideswiped what might have been a building on the right. It bounced, tilted, and started to roll over.

Though held by her seat belt, Tia was flung violently to one side. Her head struck the window frame. The glaring light went out and blackness took its place.

8

TRAP

WHEN Tia opened her eyes she found that the minibus had turned over on its top. She and the others were hanging straight down by their seat belts. She realized she couldn't have been unconscious more than a few seconds, for the wreck was still sliding over the pavement as she looked around, then it crunched slowly against a parked car and stopped.

Mr. Yokomoto, in a voice that was far from steady, called out, "Is—is everybody . . . okay?"

There were mutters and exclamations. "Yeah . . ." "Yeah—sure." "I'm okay." "You kiddin'?"

Dazzler said, "How about you, Tia?"

Tia wanted to cry. Then she wanted to sob and bawl and furiously strike her fists on something, because that man had beaten her. He had outwitted her and won and gotten away with Tony, and all she had managed to do was wreck the minibus.

"Tia?" Dazzler said worriedly.

"I—I'm fine now," she answered and dabbed at a tear that had started to run across her forehead. Somehow, no matter what, she was going to rescue Tony, and then settle accounts with that evil man and that rapacious woman who were causing so much trouble.

This resolution made, she energized the seat belts, which obligingly unbuckled themselves and allowed everyone to tumble down to the minibus ceiling, or what was left of it.

"Ump!" muttered Dazzler. "This is getting rough!"

"It's been rough!" Muscles said weakly. "I've had it."

"So's the bus," Rocky told him. "Just look at it!"

Mr. Yokomoto put a hand over his eyes. "I can't bear to look. And it's city property! Oh, no, no, no!"

The truant officer scrambled out and stood shaking his head while he tried to assess the damage.

The others followed uncertainly and gathered around Tia.

"Poor man," said Tia, looking at Mr. Yokomoto.

"Poor nothin'!" Dazzler muttered. "He's the truant officer."

Muscles whispered, "Let's get outa here before we end up in school."

They all slipped quickly away. But at the corner Tia paused and looked back. Mr. Yokomoto was still standing beside the wreck of the minibus, sadly shaking his head.

Tia swallowed. She couldn't help feeling sorry for him. After all, it was entirely her fault that the minibus was wrecked. Somehow, she resolved, she would make it up to him. Just how, she didn't know yet, but she would manage it.

• • •

That evening, in Letha Wedge's great Victorian mansion on the hill, Dr. Gannon angrily paced the library while he berated Letha and her nephew. Tony sat woodenly on one side, silent and motionless, but the inner Tony watched and listened with slowly growing uneasiness.

The doctor glared at Letha, then bit out, "You jeopardized my life's work."

"My accountants are desperate," she said lightly, lifting one shoulder.

"And you," the doctor went on, turning grimly to Sickle, "you've proved your incompetence again."

"What d'you want from me?" Sickle muttered. "I ache all over. That crazy gold was pounding me to a pulp."

Dr. Gannon swung back to Letha. He shook his head and snapped, "I don't see how I can trust you anymore."

"You don't trust me?" said Letha, raising her eyebrows. She sniffed. "I trusted you enough to make my credit rating look like Swiss cheese. When I tell you I have a problem, I don't want my ears filled with a lot of slop about Mankind and the Universe. So don't tell me you don't trust me. We have to trust each other."

"Yeah," Sickle drawled wearily. "I trust everybody."

The doctor scowled at him a moment, then turned and moved ponderously to the end of the room. Slowly he paced back and stood looking from one to the other. Finally he drew a deep breath.

"Fortunately," he began, his voice lower now, "I've worked out something very spectacular. It should satisfy us both—in prestige and money."

"You can have the prestige," Letha told him coldly. "I'll take the money. But before we celebrate your return to sanity, we'd better do something about Tony's sister. How did she know we were at the museum?"

The doctor frowned. "I'm not certain." He turned to Tony. "Tell me, Tony, how did your sister know we were at the museum?"

The inner Tony cried silently, *Don't tell him! Don't ever say anything about her!* But it had no effect at all on the captive Tony, for he replied tonelessly, like a programmed robot, "Telepathy."

"So that's it!" Letha said softly. "Ten to one says she'll show up again and ruin everything."

Dr. Gannon's face slowly hardened. "Then," he said grimly, "she'll have to be—as only you might say—scratched?"

Letha nodded.

• • •

That night in the darkness of the hideout, Tia awoke suddenly and sat up in her bunk, listening. Something had awakened her, but what? Had someone called her?

She grew tense as the call came again, and she realized she was hearing it only in her mind.

"Tia! Tia! Can you hear me?"

"Oh, Tony!" she cried happily. "I hear you! Where are you?"

"In Dr. Gannon's laboratory. Help me!"

80

"What happened to you, Tony? What made you do the awful things you did?"

"I was forced to do them. I can't explain now. Hurry!"

"But—but I don't know how to find you! What's wrong? Can't you free yourself?"

"Tia, something terrible has happened. It was something they did to me. I—I've lost my power to energize!"

"Oh, Tony! How can I find you?"

"Follow my voice path. Please!"

The urgency of his call brought her to her feet. She found her shoes, slipped into them quickly, and hurried outside.

"Okay!" she said when she reached the sidewalk. "Guide me! Which way?" She began turning in a circle, almost like a radar scanner.

"This way . . . this way . . . ," Tony began repeating.

Tia turned until she reached a point where Tony's voice seemed clearest, then ran up the street to the next corner. Again she began to turn.

"Which way now?" she asked.

"This way . . . this way . . . ," Tony repeated.

After several corrections on several streets and corners, Tia managed to fix the general direction of her destination in her mind. To reach it, she had to cross the edge of the city and then angle up into the hills. This latter part of the route was the worst, for no street led in the direction she wanted to go, most of them looping upward or winding around so that she was forced to trudge far out of her way in order to make a small gain.

Occasionally she checked on her course with Tony, and he would call back encouragingly, "You're getting closer . . ."

It was after midnight, according to her reckoning, when at last she reached the end of a drive at the top of a hill and peered uneasily upward at a great, gaunt Victorian mansion rising dark against the sky. A single streetlight illuminated the cavernous entrance. The house itself was dark, the upper part of the great structure merging with the starless blackness overhead, so that it seemed to be one with the night. Tia wouldn't have been surprised to see goblins gaping at her from the windows.

She shivered and asked, "Is this the right place?"

"Yes," Tony called. "Come inside . . . quick!"

Following it, but so faint she wasn't sure she heard it, came another call like a tiny echo. *No! No! Don't come in! Don't . . .*

Tia caught her lip between her teeth, her uneasiness rising. "Tony!" she said urgently. "Something seems wrong. What is it?"

"Everything's wrong!" came the quick reply. "Hurry! Hurry! I want to get out of here. . . . There isn't much time!"

Deciding the echo she had thought she had heard was only her imagination, she ran up the front steps and across the broad veranda to the door. She tried the knob. It was locked.

"Unlock it!" Tony said.

She energized the lock. It clicked and the door swung

open. As she entered the dark hall the door closed and locked behind her.

"Come straight ahead," Tony ordered. "There's a door under the stairway. Open it and you'll find a flight of steps going down."

By the dim glow from the streetlight that came through the hall windows, she found the door under the great curving stairway.

As her hand touched the knob she heard again the tiny echolike call. *No! No!* it urged her. *Don't come down here! Go away!*

Tia hesitated. Then her mouth firmed. The tiny echolike call was nothing but the result of her own fears. Tony was somewhere below, and he was badly in need of her help.

Determinedly she turned the knob and thrust open the door.

"Tony, are you down there?"

"Yes! Hurry before they come back!"

Reassured, she felt her way down the steps to a broad area that seemed to be a well-equipped laboratory, though it was so dimly lighted that she could see only a short distance ahead. She moved cautiously along what appeared to be the main aisle, eyes searching either side for a sign of Tony.

"Keep coming straight," Tony called. "I'm down at the end."

It was quite dark at the end, and she could make out nothing there. She stopped, her uneasiness returning.

Suddenly there was a loud baa almost in front of her. She jumped backward in quick fright, then steadied as her eyes made out the dim form of a goat peering at her with keen interest from his pen. Moving closer, she saw his name on a small sign above the gate.

Tia relaxed and smiled. She loved goats. "Hello, Alfred, you silly thing."

Alfred responded with another bleat. Immediately afterward she heard the echolike voice in her head. *I'm not as silly as most humans. You were foolish to come down here. I warned you to stay away!*

She stared at him. "Alfred!" she exclaimed. "It was you—" A telepathic goat was the last thing she had expected to find here. Not that most goats didn't have the ability, but Alfred was exceptional.

Not so loud! Alfred cautioned. *Someone may hear you. Tony—I mean the small part of him that escaped their control—has been trying to tell you to keep away from here. But his power is too weak. I can barely hear him myself. I promised him I'd tell you—*

"But—but where is he?" she whispered.

At the end of the aisle, tied to a chair. He—

"Tia!" Tony called. "Help me!"

She took a step forward, peering into the darkness. Now, as her eyes became more accustomed to the gloom, she could make out the helpless figure of Tony fastened securely to a heavy chair. It was astonishing to see him a prisoner there, powerless to unfasten the cords that any child at Witch Mountain could have dealt with in seconds.

She started to run toward him and energize the cords, but abruptly a warning from Alfred flashed into her mind: *Get away from here! Hurry! Hurry!*

84

Tia hesitated. She half turned, uncertain. There was a movement out of the darkness behind her, and suddenly a large hand pressed a cloth over her mouth and nose.

She twisted around, fighting. For a moment the face of the driver of the black car, teeth gritted, filled her vision. Then as she struggled for breath the driver's face became distorted and blurred, and everything went black.

9

MISSION FOR ALFRED

AS TIA SLUMPED, unconscious, in Sickle's firm grasp, the lights came on in the laboratory and Letha Wedge and Dr. Gannon stepped through the side door and hurried down the aisle.

"Well, I've got her," Sickle muttered, as if somehow the task had been distasteful to him. "Now what do you want me to do with her?"

"Bring her over here," said the doctor, stopping by the main operating table. "We'll take care of her."

Sickle lifted Tia, carried her to the table, and placed her upon it. He stepped aside and stood watching while his aunt and the doctor strapped her down carefully and blindfolded her.

Finally Dr. Gannon nodded to him and said, "Bring me one of the plastic cases. Make it the large one we use for the bigger animals."

Sickle went to a storage unit, selected a heavy, transparent plastic case, and brought it to the table. When it was placed over Tia, covering her from head to foot, it formed an airtight chamber. Now gas cylinders were rolled to the table, and hoses from these were connected to the case.

Dr. Gannon adjusted the valves and stood back, looking grimly at his victim.

"This will keep her," he said.

"Keep her for what?" Sickle muttered uneasily.

"For you to dispose of later," the doctor told him, smiling thinly. "In the meantime it will keep her from interfering with our plans."

"I need a drink," said Letha, heading for the door. "This has been a day."

The others followed her, forgetting Tony and turning the lights off.

The captive Tony, fastened to his chair, had watched the entire episode with no more change of expression than a store window mannequin. But the inner Tony had raged. He was still raging when the others left.

I'm sorry, Alfred told him. *I did my best to make her leave, but she was too worried about you.*

We've got to do something! Tony agonized. *We can't just let her die . . .*

She won't die. Not till the doctor is ready for her to. Anyway, there is nothing we can do tonight. She is unconscious, and I am chained in my pen.

Can't you break your chain?

Perhaps. I have considered it. But one needs a motive greater than self to break chains. Possibly, for her sake . . .

I don't see how you can stand it, being a prisoner here.

If you had been born a goat, Alfred reminded him, *you would have learned to philosophize and take life as it comes.*

87

But I am not a goat.

More the pity. From what I have seen of humans, I would rather be a goat than any human on this planet.

But I am not from this planet, the inner Tony said miserably. *I'm from another world where people would never dream of treating each other the way they do here.*

Well! Alfred exclaimed. *That explains it. I'd wondered why you and your sister were the only people I've ever been able to exchange an intelligent thought with. A pity we are forced to meet under such uncomfortable circumstances, when I am chained, and you are bottled up in yourself, so to speak.*

Alfred paused a moment, then said, *Now, about this unhappy situation. A shame your regular self cannot take orders from a goat, for I would order you to shake off your bonds and free your sister, then take to your heels as soon as she is awake and can walk. But no, that is impossible. So let us consider the possible. Has your sister any friends?*

I—I think so. At least I saw her with a bunch of boys at the museum, and it seemed as if they were trying to help her.

Who are they?

I don't know.

Then we will have to wait till she wakes up, and ask her. In the meantime I shall take a bit of rest so I will be ready for the trials of tomorrow. I suggest you do the same.

How can I possibly rest with the way things are? the inner Tony asked plaintively.

You are a worrier, so that's your worry. I am a philosopher, so I will sleep.

88

• • •

The darkness of the laboratory was beginning to gray when the inner Tony became aware of low, incoherent sounds coming from the plastic case that covered Tia.

Alfred! he called. *Alfred! I think she's coming out of it!*

I'm awake, said Alfred and gave a loud bleat to prove it. *But do not count on her coming entirely out of it. I did not see fit to mention it last night, but one of those cylinders attached to her case contains gas. The doctor's intention, I'm sure, is to keep her far enough under so she cannot make use of those curious powers you two seem to possess.*

That's what I've been afraid of, Tony admitted. *But I didn't want to think about it. I don't know what we'll do if she can't talk to us.*

Tia's mumbling was becoming more distinct. "Tony . . . ," she was repeating weakly. "Crusher . . . Muscles . . . Alfred . . . Where am I? . . . Alfred . . ."

At the sound of his name, Alfred, who had been comfortably relaxed on his bed of hay, stood up abruptly, his long ears twitching forward.

"Alfred . . . ," Tia continued in her weak, faraway voice. "Alfred . . . help—help me!"

Alfred bleated to let her know she had been heard and strained forward to the end of his chain. He gave a few experimental tugs, then backed up a few paces. Now, lowering his head, he gave a powerful lunge forward. The chain snapped as if it had been a string.

With another bleat, Alfred trotted out of his pen and

over to the side of the heavy table where Tia lay imprisoned under the plastic case.

He pressed his nose against the side of the case and bleated again to announce his presence. *I am here to help,* he told her. *Have you friends I can bring here?*

"Friends . . . yes . . . the Earthquakes . . ."

The Earthquakes? Alfred repeated, not sure what she meant. *They are friends?*

"Yes. Rocky . . . Muscles . . . Crusher . . . Dazzler . . . They are . . . the Earthquakes. . . . Find them. . . ."

Where are they?

"At their . . . hideout . . . down in . . . city . . . old part . . . old house . . . sort of . . . like this . . ."

As she mumbled the words, Alfred caught a hazy vision of the Earthquakes' hideout from her mind and an even hazier vision of the street it was on. He was about to ask for more detailed information when he heard footsteps beyond the side door, quickly approaching from the back hall. He recognized the impatient tread of Dr. Gannon.

I'll find them! Alfred said hurriedly and sprang down the aisle toward the steps under the great stairway near the main entrance. He scrambled to the top of them, butted the door open, and spun into the front hall.

The big front door, he knew, was locked, but he wasted no time with it. Lowering his big curved horns, he sprang forward, smashed through the lower panel, and trotted out on the porch.

At the edge of it he paused a moment, sniffing the good air of freedom and enjoying his first sight of the

90

sun in many months. It was just coming up over a distant hill. He gave it a healthy baa of greeting, then started down toward the city spread out below. He had a feeling this was going to be a really fine day.

• • •

As Alfred started down the hill to begin his search, the four Earthquakes picked their way around to the side of the old monstrosity they thought of as their own, and entered their hideout.

"Hey, Tia!" Crusher called, forgetting at this hour to speak out of the side of his mouth. "Tia! We got some cold hot cakes for you!"

He stopped abruptly. The others halted beside him, looking with surprise around at the empty room.

"She—she ain't here!" Rocky muttered uneasily.

Muscles set down the half-empty bottle of syrup he had lifted from his mother's kitchen and stood rubbing his thin arms while he frowned at her empty bunk. He shook his head. "I sure hope she didn't go lookin' for Tony without us. She could get in trouble."

"Yeah," said Dazzler. "She needs us."

Crusher placed the cold hot cakes on the table by the syrup and went over and felt Tia's bunk. "It's cold," he said. "She musta been gone a long time. Wonder why she left."

"She musta got a clue," said Dazzler.

"Yeah, but where did it take her?" Crusher asked.

"Only person can answer that is Tia," said Dazzler.

They looked at each other helplessly and finally sat

down. For a while no one had anything to say.

At last Rocky ventured, "Looks like we oughta do something."

"You name it," said Muscles.

"Well, we sure can't find her by staying here," Rocky insisted.

"I don't see why not," Muscles told him. "It's the best place to find her. She's bound to come back here. All we got to do is wait."

"Okay," Rocky admitted. "I'd just as soon stay. It sure beats goin' to school!"

• • •

Alfred, by this time, had reached the bottom of the hill and was traveling at a fast clip toward a school intersection where a patrolman had just brought traffic to a halt. The cars ahead of him stopped, bumper to bumper, but Alfred saw no reason for wasting time by lingering in the rear. A perfectly good path led to the crossing.

A nimble leap took him to the trunk of the first car he came to. From here he proceeded across the roof to the front, and was about to step down on the hood when curiosity prompted him to lower his head and peer through the windshield. He saw nothing but a plump woman in diamonds painting her lips before the rear-view mirror. At the sight of him she did a double take, screamed, and dove to the floor, smearing lipstick over her face.

Alfred, in disgust, went on across the hood and was

about to leap to the trunk of the next car when he wondered what it was about him that had frightened the woman. He glanced back and caught his reflection in the windshield. It couldn't be my horns, he thought. She should have admired them instead of acting so idiotic. I'm not vain, but it's really a fine set. They don't come finer.

Suddenly wondering what the occupants of the next car would think of them, he hopped to the trunk ahead of him and climbed to the roof. Quickly crossing the roof he reached the hood and glanced back. His sudden appearance brought anything but admiration. Instead there was consternation and a sudden wild scramble from the front seat to the back one.

Alfred snorted in really high disgust and leaped to the crosswalk. "Baa!" he said to the patrolman, who waved a stop sign at him. "Baa! Baa! Baaaa!" He lowered his horns, which really were formidable, and had no trouble whatever in clearing the patrolman from his path.

At least, he thought, as he gained the opposite corner and started down a more interesting street, if humans don't admire a fine set of horns, they do have respect for them.

Then, thinking of his mission and the probable location of the hideout where he hoped to find the Earthquakes, he realized that much valuable time might be lost if he depended solely upon his cloven feet to take him there. Tia could easily die if he were too slow in bringing aid.

At that moment, on the next corner ahead, he saw a man flagging down a taxi. In sudden inspiration, he changed from a fast trot to a charging gallop.

He didn't think much of taxis or the humans that used them, but there are times, he had learned, that even a goat must be resourceful and take every possible advantage, if he hoped to reach his destination.

10

MISSION IN PROGRESS

ALFRED, in his eagerness to reach the taxi before it picked up its fare and left, was moving at top speed by the time he reached the corner. The fare, Alfred saw, was a self-important-looking man of the type who likes to give orders. He had just opened the door and was about to step inside the cab when Alfred crossed the curb.

Had the fare been a quiet little old lady in black, Alfred instinctively would have made a slight change in direction and landed neatly on the taxi's trunk. But the fare was a man in expensive clothes, with an air about him that put Alfred in mind of Dr. Gannon, so he merely lowered his horns and kept going.

The resulting impact sent the man straight into the taxi and out through the door on the other side. Alfred finished in complete control of the seat, nor did he object when the taxi pulled away with a jerk that automatically closed both doors.

By one of those curious chances which even the fates have never satisfactorily explained, the driver of the taxi was none other than the impatient Eddie, who had run out of gas with Tony and Tia.

Eddie, without a backward glance, put the flag down and said, "Did you tell me Fourth and Market, sir?"

Alfred expressed his immediate opinion of the cabby with a snort.

"Yes, sir," said Eddie. "I'll have you there in a couple minutes, sir."

"Baa!" said Alfred.

"Yes, sir," said Eddie, leaning over the wheel and concentrating on his driving. "Feel the power of this cab?"

"Baa!" Alfred repeated.

"But it's got plenty of power!" Eddie protested. "Everybody tells me I oughta be a race driver. What do you think?"

"Baa!" said Alfred again, which expressed his true opinion better than words.

"Well, I think you're wrong!" Eddie flung back, his voice rising. "I'm one of the best cabbies in this part of the country. Anybody'll tell you that. I got all the makings of a race driver. I'll show you!"

The taxi began weaving in and out of traffic like a frightened rabbit pursued by hounds, speed increasing at every chance. This made no difference at all to Alfred, so long as the taxi continued to move in the right general direction.

"Now don't you worry about nothin'," said Eddie, narrowly missing a truck and giving a pedestrian the fright of his life. "I'm a safe driver. Want me to tell you how safe I am?"

"Baa!" said Alfred wearily and wished the cabby would keep his mouth shut. The human voice, in his opinion, left much to be desired and could hardly be compared to the musical bleating of a herd of goats.

"Well, I'll tell you anyway," Eddie persisted. "I been hackin' nineteen years, eleven months. In all that time I never even scratched a cab. Next month they're gonna give me the gold safety award. What do you think of that?"

"Baa!" Alfred said automatically.

Eddie grunted. "You don't like nothin'! I sure hope you're a good tipper."

"Baa!" said Alfred lustily.

Eddie muttered something under his breath, and added, "I knew there was something about you that didn't look right." Frowning, he glanced in the rearview mirror, and for the first time saw Alfred's head framed in it.

A strange expression crossed Eddie's face. He picked up a rag and wiped off the mirror, then glanced into it again. He swallowed, and his eyes and mouth opened wide. Abruptly he spun around and looked squarely at Alfred.

"Baa!" said Alfred, in great enjoyment, then braced himself when he saw where the untended taxi was heading.

There was a shuddering impact as the taxi slammed into the rear of another car. Following it came the sound of metal parts falling to the paving.

Eddie, shocked and trembling, staggered out and jerked open the rear door, which fell off with a clatter.

"Get outa my cab!" he yelled. "Out! Out!"

Alfred gave a final baa and hopped nimbly out. At the sight of him and his formidable horns, the gathering onlookers quickly scattered and allowed him all the trotting room he needed. He heard Eddie moaning about his perfect record, but he did not look back.

At the next corner Alfred paused and looked carefully to the left and to the right. The hideout had to be somewhere near. He could feel it. He decided the best way to find it would be to follow his nose and let intuition take him around the proper corner. Had there been another honest creature around, instead of streams of ordinary humans, he could have mentally asked directions. But there wasn't even a pigeon he could pass the time of day with. You could do nothing with a human except give him the old baa treatment, or lower your horns at the right moment.

Alfred closed his eyes, tested the air, then opened them and turned sharply to the left. Far down, where the street curved through an area of general dilapidation, he saw an old building that seemed to answer the description Tia had given him.

He gave a baa for luck and to clear the way and set off down the street at a fast trot.

• • •

At the hideout the Earthquakes were sitting disconsolately around, saying nothing while Muscles tested a cold hot cake.

Muscles said glumly, "I can't figure where she went. You know her. . . . She coulda went anywhere."

Dazzler turned at a sound outside. "Hear that?" he said. "Must be her now."

Rocky sprang up hopefully, hurried to the door, and

98

opened it. He stiffened and his mouth came open.

Before him stood Alfred.

"Baa!" said Alfred, by way of greeting.

Rocky jumped back with a yell of fright. "Watch out!" he cried.

Alfred snorted and charged into the room. The frightened Earthquakes scattered in every direction, climbing the walls and furniture. Alfred baaed with delight and climbed after them. It was fun for a moment, then he realized he was getting nowhere and began running from one to the other, giving anxious little baas while he looked earnestly into their faces.

"It's a monster!" Crusher gasped. "What's the matter with him? Is he crazy?"

"He's a crazy wild beast!" Rocky cried.

"Oh, Tia!" Muscles wailed. "Where are you when we need you?"

Alfred confronted Dazzler, baaing earnestly.

Dazzler said, "He keeps lookin' at me like he knows me!"

Alfred gave a happy baa and nodded his head.

"What do you want from me?" asked Dazzler.

Alfred gave a louder baa and trotted to the door. Then he stopped and turned and looked entreatingly from one boy to the other.

"Maybe he's hungry," Rocky said.

"Don't give him the hot cakes," Muscles said quickly.

Alfred went to each boy, trotting to the door every time and then turning.

Crusher said, "It's like he wants us to go outside with him."

Dazzler shook his head. "I don't wanna go outside with *that* thing!"

Alfred was suddenly worried. How could he get these boys away from here and on the run for Dr. Gannon's laboratory? He looked around the room and saw a sweater hanging over a chair. Tia's? He trotted up to it and quickly grabbed it in his mouth when he recognized Tia's scent. With a bound he was out of the door and running with it.

"Stop him!" Crusher yelled. "He's got Tia's sweater!"

"He's gonna eat it!" Muscles cried, rushing to the door.

"Hurry!" Dazzler gasped, following Muscles. "Take it away from him!"

They dashed after him, trying to snatch the sweater from him before he reached the sidewalk. But Alfred charged through the rubble, crossed the sidewalk well ahead of them, and began running up the middle of the street.

The four boys followed, yelling, while traffic stopped and pedestrians and drivers gaped.

• • •

It was a long run back to Letha Wedge's towering mansion, most of it uphill. Alfred slowed his pace only when he saw his pursuers were tiring and allowed them to almost catch up with him before he bounded ahead. In spite of aching muscles and straining lungs, the Earthquakes kept doggedly behind him, and not once was there talk of giving up the chase.

By the time Alfred reached the mansion steps, his

100

opinion of the four pursuers had gone up considerably. He ran to the top of the steps, paused just long enough for the Earthquakes to come bounding after him, then charged the partially destroyed door and smashed through to the hall.

The dogged Earthquakes followed closely. They were right behind him when he clattered downward under the great stairway and arrived in the laboratory below. By this time Alfred was almost fond of them.

Everyone stopped, breathing rapidly from the long run. They looked curiously around.

When he had got his breath, Muscles said in a low voice, "Hey . . . this is some kinda science place."

"Let's get outa here!" said Rocky.

"Not till we get Tia's sweater," Crusher told him.

Suddenly Dazzler pointed and said excitedly, "Hey . . . Look!"

They all turned and stared. Ahead of them, under the plastic case, strapped to the table and blindfolded, was Tia.

Rocky shouted, and they ran to the table.

"Quick!" said Dazzler. "Let's get her outa there!"

Two of them moved to each side of the case, and very carefully they lifted it off and dropped it on the floor.

"Tia!" said Muscles. "Tia!"

"Phew!" Crusher gasped. "It smells!"

"Must be some kinda gas!" said Dazzler, as they backed away. "Come on . . . hold your breath. We gotta untie her!"

With Alfred watching and baaing, they unfastened the straps that bound Tia and carried her to an open spot on the floor. Muscles removed her blindfold, and

101

Dazzler hurried to a sink, tried the faucet, and came back with a glass of water. They crowded around and supported her while she drank from the glass. Finally she was able to sit up and look about.

"You okay now?" asked Dazzler.

"I—I'm much better now," Tia managed to say. "Thank you . . . thank you so much . . ."

"How'd you get here?" Muscles asked.

"Tony . . . he was calling me. He guided me here. It—it was late last night when I got here . . . and Tony . . ." She sat up straight and looked around. Suddenly she pointed to a chair at the end of the aisle. "He—he was tied in that chair, but where is he now?"

Rocky shrugged. "You askin' us?"

All at once Tia put her hands to her face. "I—I see something!" she exclaimed.

They came close again. "What . . . where . . . ?"

"A big . . . round . . . thing!" she said. "That's where Tony is! I'm sure of it! Big and round!"

"Like a ball?" said Crusher. "A great big ball?"

"Yes!"

"I know where it is!" Crusher told her.

"Then let's go!" she cried. "Hurry!"

She sprang up and they ran for the stairs. Halfway there she heard Alfred baa behind her. She stopped and rushed back.

"Oh, Alfred," she said, putting her arms around his neck and kissing him. "Thank you for everything. Hold down the fort till we find Tony, and we'll be back!"

"Baa!" said Alfred happily and added mentally, *Good luck!*

II

PLUTONIUM

WHILE Tia and the Earthquakes were hurrying to find him, Tony was being driven out of the city on a long winding trip into the hills. At a word from Dr. Gannon, Sickle pulled off the road at the top of a hill and parked the car under a group of trees. Everyone got out.

The captive Tony moved woodenly at the doctor's bidding, as docile as a lamb; but the inner Tony eyed Gannon with ever-rising hate and again tried to contact Alfred, even though he knew it was useless. Alfred's range was entirely too short, as was his own at the moment. He had been amazingly lucky just to contact Alfred in the first place, but how had it all come out? Where was Alfred now? Had he managed to get help, and had Tia been freed?

The awful part of it was not knowing. The incredible part was that he and Tia, in spite of abilities that should have protected them from creatures like the doctor and his greedy friend, had fallen into their clutches.

Buzzards! he thought, and again wondered what the pair of them were up to this morning. Earlier, just after Alfred had gone for help, Dr. Gannon had come into the laboratory, ordered him to free himself, and then get cleaned up for breakfast. Afterward he had been told to lie down on his cot and rest till further orders.

"I've a big task for you today," the doctor had said. "I want you to be thoroughly rested and fresh for it."

Why didn't you think of that last night? he had raged inwardly. *But no, you left me tied up in a chair till dawn.*

Tony hoped he would make a rousing mess of everything the doctor ordered him to do. After all, with only a two-hour nap. But no, it wouldn't be that way. His race, from the planet of the double suns, had many times the endurance of earthborn people.

As the captive Tony followed Dr. Gannon to the crest of the hill, the inner Tony looked curiously ahead, wondering what was in store for him. Stretching below was a factory complex whose odd-shaped buildings set it entirely apart from the average industrial group. It was surrounded by a high steel fence whose only entrance was at a gatehouse where armed guards were on duty.

"What kind of place is that?" asked Sickle, scowling at it.

Dr. Gannon paused for a moment, and said quietly, "It's an underground plutonium processing plant."

"Huh?" said Sickle.

"It's where U-235 becomes Pu-239."

Sickle gave a little shake of his head, and Letha Wedge said, "Translate that into financial terms, Victor."

"Plutonium, my dear, is considerably more valuable than gold."

Letha Wedge smiled. "That's what I like about science: They're always discovering more expensive things."

Sickle asked, "What's so good about this plutonium?"

"If you'd change your reading habits, you wouldn't have to ask such a question," the doctor said dryly. "It's used as the explosive core of nuclear missile warheads —if that's what you call good."

"And I suppose," Letha Wedge said lightly, "you'll have Tony whip up an atom bomb or something?" She started to laugh, but sobered quickly when she saw the stony expression on Dr. Gannon's face. A corner of her mouth twitched nervously.

The doctor gave her a hard look and slowly nodded. "In effect, yes. That's what Tony is here for. Plutonium is a powerful, lethal radioactive element. We'll take over the atomic reactor where its's processed, cause a chain reaction explosion, which will release a radioactive cloud that will drift from city to city."

She gasped. "I—I didn't count on killing anyone, Victor. Especially us. It's not a good idea."

"Oh, it'll never go that far," the doctor assured her. "They'll pay anything to prevent it. Do you think five million dollars might spread some joy among your accountants?"

Letha rolled her eyes. "It'll blow the transistors clear out of their calculators."

The doctor smiled. Hands on hips, head raised imperially, he looked around like a potentate surveying his domain.

"This," he said, "is the first step in making myself the most powerful man in the world."

• • •

The inner Tony was so shocked by Dr. Gannon's plan that he was hardly aware of getting back into the car and being driven down to the gatehouse in front of the plutonium plant.

Monster! he thought. *Greedy monster! And you want to use me to do all this! Me!*

Somehow he had to stop it. But how? How could he, bottled up like this and powerless, do anything at all? Come to think of it, he wasn't entirely helpless. He had managed to get Alfred's attention, and that had started something. Maybe, if he kept trying, he could come up with a thought that would upset the doctor's apple-cart. . . .

He was concentrating so hard that he failed to hear the doctor's instructions to the captive Tony as they approached the gatehouse. What happened came as a complete surprise, even though a part of himself was responsible for it.

The gatehouse was a small affair in the center of the entrance, with a lift gate on either side. As Sickle drove up to it on the right, a truck coming out of the plant stopped on the other side, its radio playing loudly. A guard leaned out to check the truck driver's papers. He okayed them, then signaled for the gate to be lifted. As it went up, the truck began to move and the guard leaned out to check the doctor's car.

"What can I do for you folks?" the guard said politely.

"You can take a powder," Letha told him. At the same time the doctor touched the captive Tony on the

106

shoulder and gave a nod of command.

Instantly the entire gatehouse, with the guard inside, rose into the air, moved over a few feet, and was deposited neatly on the back of the truck as it moved away. As the truck sped off down the road, the inner Tony got a glimpse of the guard trying desperately to get out and yelling for help. But the truck's radio was playing so loudly it seemed doubtful that anyone could hear him.

Sickle, at a word from the doctor, sent the car forward, headed directly for the plant.

Dr. Gannon pointed to a tower on the hill behind the main building. "Tony," he ordered, "that is the outer security scanner. Put it out of commission—permanently."

No! the inner Tony cried silently, with all the power he could muster. *Don't do it! Don't follow his orders!*

If the captive Tony heard this inner plea, he paid not the slightest attention to it. For all at once it seemed as if a stray bolt of lightning must have struck the tower. A great shower of sparks exploded from the top, and suddenly the entire tower crumpled and fell down the hill. This brought an instant reaction from the interior of the building, for flashes of sparks glittered through the windows, and excited guards rushed outside, pointing at the toppled tower.

The inner Tony was appalled. As he visualized what was soon to follow, he wished he could flee back into some remote corner of his skull and hide.

Sickle brought the car to a quick stop near the building. Directly ahead a concrete stairway led downward to a lower level. At a sharp word from the doctor, everyone got out and moved swiftly down the stairway toward a door. Before they reached it, the door suddenly swung open and two guards rushed out on the double. The doctor's group had just time to flatten themselves against the wall as the guards went past and ran up the stairway.

Dr. Gannon, with one hand on Tony, led the way through the door, across an entrance hall, and down another stairway. As they started downward, the inner Tony squirmed as he read the sign on the wall to his left: PLUTONIUM FURNACE.

At the foot of the stairway they reached a long corridor. At the end of it was a steel door marked: FURNACE ROOM. The doctor, with his hand still firmly on Tony's shoulder, moved swiftly toward the steel door. Letha Wedge and Sickle, lips tight, followed close behind them.

Just before they reached the door, a stern-faced security guard appeared suddenly from a recess on the left. A plastic tag on his jacket indicated that his name was Dolan.

"Wait a minute," Dolan ordered in a firm voice. "You can't go in there without an I.D."

Dr. Gannon smiled at him. He gave Tony's shoulder a quick squeeze, and said, "Tony, show him our I.D."

The inner Tony cried a soundless protest, but the captive Tony made short work of levitating the security guard and flattening him against the ceiling.

The astounded Dolan struggled helplessly to get down. "Wha-what's happened?" he gasped. "W-where? How? What?"

They passed under the suspended guard and stopped before the steel door.

"Tony," said Dr. Gannon, "open the door."

No! shrieked the inner Tony and pounded nonexistent fists against the walls enclosing him. *No! No! No! Don't do anything he says from now on!*

For the first time the captive Tony seemed to hesitate, but it was for only a second or two. He concentrated on the heavy steel door. Slowly it opened.

Dr. Gannon, with Tony at his side, went through into the furnace room. The others followed.

"Now, Tony," the doctor ordered, "seal the door so that no one can open it."

Tony energized the great door. Slowly it swung closed. Now, as they turned and moved forward, the inner Tony was aware of a humming sound coming from the huge reactor ahead of them. It reached him as a deadly sound, filling him with a terrible apprehension.

Dr. Gannon paused. Hands on hips, he looked about with an imperial gesture. "My friends," he said, his voice vibrating as if he felt the moment was a dramatic one, "we are about to make scientific history."

Now he turned to Tony and pointed to the big control panel on his right. "Tony," he ordered in the same dramatic tone, "shut down the complete cooling system, including the emergency backup system!"

At the order, the inner Tony went wild. With all the power he could muster, he shrieked, *No! No! No! Don't you dare! This is a terrible thing! NO! NO! NO!*

Again the captive Tony hesitated, as if somewhere in the very remote distance he had heard a faint dissenting voice. But the voice was much too small and far too remote to have any real effect upon the given order.

He concentrated on the control panel.

• • •

All over the plant various pieces of machinery slowed and suddenly came to a stop. In the control room, warning lights began to flash on the console. The ever-watchful monitor blinked at the panel in surprise and some uneasiness.

"Hey, we've got red lights on the cooling system," he announced.

The operations officer hurried over and studied the panel. "Probably it's only a circuit breaker," he muttered. "Restart the system."

The monitor pressed several buttons. Nothing happened. Again he tried it. Again there was no response.

The monitor shook his head worriedly. "I can't get a restart!"

"Hit the backup system," said the operations officer.

With his lip between his teeth, the monitor punched a new series of buttons. Once again nothing happened.

The monitor swallowed and said tensely, "I've got a no-go on the backup!"

Beyond them an engineer turned from a meter and called sharply, "I've got the temperature increasing! Let's get that coolant flowing!"

Face tightening, the engineer turned back to his meter. His jaws clenched as he saw that the temperature was steadily rising.

The telephone rang, and the operations officer snatched it up. "Reactor control . . ."

Down in the furnace room it was Dr. Gannon who was making the call while the others stood close, listening.

"Control?" said the doctor. "You don't really think you're controlling anything, do you?"

"Who—who is this?" demanded the operations officer.

"I am Doctor Victor Gannon," the doctor began slowly, in the grand manner of one addressing a large audience, "until this moment known only to a small segment of the scientific community. From this time forward, I'll be known to the entire world."

"Yeah?" snapped the operations officer. "Look. I don't know what you're talking about, but I haven't time to fool—"

"I've shut down your cooling system," the doctor interrupted in a loud voice.

"Okay. . . . If you've shut it down, then put it back on!"

"Victor," Letha Wedge said quickly, "tell him how expensive it will be to put it back on."

Dr. Gannon said, "The temperature in the reactor is getting hot, hot, hotter. In about an hour we'll be serving grilled plutonium, medium rare, to the atmosphere . . . unless the following conditions are met."

"W-what conditions?"

"Within the hour," the doctor told him, "five million dollars cash . . . a jet waiting at the airport . . . safe escort. Most importantly, you will announce that Doctor Victor Gannon has achieved molecular control and mind control, and that this is the first in a series of worldwide demonstrations of his power. Those wishing to align themselves with me should make their intentions known."

He hung up and put a possessive arm around Tony.

111

"Soon," he said expansively, "we'll not only be sitting on top of the world, we'll own it."

Letha Wedge gave what was intended to be a smile. "How long, Victor, does it take to count five million dollars?"

• • •

The inner Tony was just beginning to recover from his furious expenditure of energy, and his dismal failure to prevent what was happening now. For a moment he almost wished he could be philosophical like Alfred and take life as it comes. But that was impossible for him. He didn't come from a race that would ever accept defeat or slavery, and he wasn't about to accept it now.

The trouble was that he had so little to fight with. Just his thoughts alone. And his thoughts, coming from such a small part of him and bottled up as he was, could hardly generate enough energy to keep a gnat on the prowl.

Still, he had twice made the captive Tony hesitate. The second hesitation had been longer than the first, so he had gained a little.

But it had been costly. The second time it had taken all the energy he could muster to slow the captive Tony down by a few seconds, and afterward he had sort of blanked out for a while. Still, what mattered the cost if he could cause a delay?

A delay, he suddenly realized, a delay of only a second or two—if it came at the right time—could easily mean victory for himself and the end of Dr. Gannon.

The thing to do now was to watch and listen, and be

112

ready if an opportunity came.

Matters were already moving swiftly to a head. Somewhere a siren was beginning to wail a warning. There were sounds as if security guards were struggling to open the big steel door. Nor was it hard to imagine the excitement and fear throughout the entire plant as the deadly temperature in the reactor continued to rise to the explosive point. Probably, at this very moment, orders were being given to evacuate the area and to put the city on the alert.

12

RED ALERT

THE INNER TONY was entirely right about what was happening in other parts of the plant. Besides going a little bit mad from tension—for it needed but a few more degrees of heat, and there would be nothing left to worry about—everyone was trying desperately to get stalled machinery going again, to take the proper actions before it was too late.

At an emergency meeting in the control room with the executives and the chief of staff, the operations officer was saying, "We still don't know how it happened. I just hope to heaven we can stop it from blowing in time. Are we going to pay them, Mr. Clearcole?"

Mr. Clearcole, the chief of staff, was struggling to be calm. His big hand closed into a fist on the table, and he nodded. "We'll have to pay the rascals. There's no other way. Evacuate the area immediately, and put Los Angeles on the alert!"

• • •

Miles away on the edge of the city, Tia still had no idea of what was really happening. She had had the mental flash of a huge round ball-like thing in which Tony was somehow concerned, and Crusher, who seemed to know what it was, was hurrying to lead her to it.

Crusher rounded a corner, and Tia and the other Earthquakes followed, panting for breath. Crusher suddenly stopped and pointed excitedly.

"There it is!" he cried. "There's the ball!"

They all stared at a huge golf ball perched on a giant tee, which was being used to advertise a golf school and a driving range.

The boys looked anxiously at Tia. "Is that it?" Muscles asked.

Tia swallowed in disappointment and shook her head. "No," she said, fighting to hold back her tears. If they didn't find Tony soon, it might cost him his life. "It—it was even bigger," she added.

The boys shoved Crusher in frustration. "Aw, leave me alone!" he muttered. "I was only tryin'!"

Then something caught his eye across the street. He pointed and gasped, "Hey, look!"

Everyone turned and stared through the open gate of an auto wrecking yard, which was opposite the golf school. Parked near the entrance were the sad remains of the school minibus. Mr. Yokomoto, moving like a man in a daze, was slowly removing his personal belongings, while the bus radio blared raucously away. In sudden anger Mr. Yokomoto struck the radio with his fist, but it continued to play. Then, turning, he suddenly caught sight of them.

"Oh, no!" said Rocky fearfully. "Let's get outa here!"

As he started to run, Mr. Yokomoto looked over at them, shook his head a little sadly, and waved them off. The other Earthquakes, on the point of flight, relaxed when they realized he was not going to chase them.

Dazzler shouted, "Whatsa matter, Mr. Yoyo? Don't you wanna ketch us?"

Mr. Yokomoto gave them a sour look. "It's not my job anymore. I've been fired. They're on their way down here to give me the pink slip. All because I was trying to help you kids."

Again he struck at the radio, harder this time. The only effect was to make it play louder.

Tia stood looking at the bulldoggish little man. She couldn't help feeling sorry for him.

Muscles said, "I don't trust him. He's just tryin' to use some kinda psychology trick on us."

"I believe him," she told him. "But everything that's happened is my fault. I've got to apologize to him."

She crossed over into the wrecking yard. The Earthquakes stood watching her a moment, then followed uncertainly.

Tia went up to the truant officer and said, "Mr. Yokomoto, I'm awfully sorry about what happened. I'll be glad to fix it."

The little man shook his head. "You've already fixed the bus, and my career as well. So don't fix anything else."

He shook his head again, and sighed. "All I ever wanted out of life was someday to have all the kids I put back in school come and visit me, and say, 'Thanks, Mr. Yoyo . . . er . . . Yokomoto. If it wasn't for you making

116

me get an education, I'd be a creep today.' That's all I ever wanted."

Mr. Yokomoto turned away and began taking some things out of the glove compartment.

The Earthquakes looked sheepishly at the truant officer, and then at each other.

Muscles said, "I told you he was gonna hit us with some heavy psychology. I mean, I feel sorta guilty!"

There was a sudden blare of static on the bus radio. Mr. Yokomoto banged it angrily with his fist. Immediately there came the voice of a newscaster:

"The danger to the city of radioactive fallout is increasing. . . . Experts are baffled as to how this condition mysteriously came about."

"Radios!" Mr. Yokomoto grumbled. "If it isn't bad music, it's bad news."

He was about to bang it again when Tia cried, "Wait!"

". . . An official describes the atomic reactor controls as seeming to be frozen in position, as if, quote-unquote, the molecular flow had been interrupted."

Tia put her hand over her forehead as abruptly there came to her a clearer view of the plutonium plant.

"Tony!" she whispered.

Everyone looked around at her. "What? . . . Where?" Dazzler asked.

"On the radio!" she told him. "Listen!"

"Unless the demands of the terrorists are met, the reactor will explode with the force of ten megatons. The plutonium plant is being evacuated."

Tia cried, "That's where he is! We've got to go there! As fast as we can!"

Mr. Yokomoto blinked at her. "Your truant brother —he is about to cause a radioactive holocaust?"

"It won't happen if we can get there in time." While she spoke she was looking desperately around at the wrecked cars.

Muscles said, "How we gonna get there in time? I mean, what are we gonna do . . . take a bus?"

Tia's frantically searching eyes settled on the minibus. Anxiously she studied it. All at once she said, "We'll go in that!"

Lips compressed, she went over to the battered remains of the minibus and touched it with her hand.

A slow grinding sound was heard as the starter began to turn. It was agonizing to listen to it.

"Hey . . . ," Mr. Yokomoto said uneasily. "What—what is this?"

The motor choked, then it began to gasp and wheeze as the starter continued to crank it. Suddenly black smoke was pouring from the exhaust pipe.

Rocky cried, "Tia's doing it again!"

Now everyone crowded around the minibus. Mr. Yokomoto could only stare at it with his mouth hanging open, beyond words.

Tia, concentrating, put her other hand to the front of the motor. It burst into life with a loud, painful sound, vibrating and trembling violently. But second by second the sound became stronger and steadier.

Crusher burst out, "Hey, Tia! We got two flats!"

She turned and looked as he pointed at the flat tires, and she energized them quickly.

As they inflated, Mr. Yokomoto stared at them, then kicked one and looked at Tia. "How . . . how . . . how?"

Tia cried, "It's ready! Hurry!"

The Earthquakes dragged and pushed Mr. Yokomoto aboard and got in themselves through whatever openings they could find. The little man protested loudly, but found himself thrust into the driver's seat. The transmission began to grind, and with Tia's help slid into gear. Abruptly the minibus leaped forward.

"Oh, no! No!" Mr. Yokomoto cried. "It's happening again!"

Shaking and chugging, the battered minibus roared into the street. It jumped ahead spasmodically at first, but as it picked up speed it began weaving precariously in and out of traffic, going faster and faster.

Truck drivers, hearing the strange roar of its approach, looked around apprehensively and gasped in disbelief as the dented wreck shot past. It was gone almost before they could see it, easily dodging oncoming vehicles and leaping safely into openings that hardly seemed to exist.

Mr. Yokomoto, clutching the wheel with white-knuckled hands but not really controlling it, was more terrified than he had ever been. He was constantly closing his eyes when it seemed that a crash was inevitable. His foot, jumping ineffectively from the accelerator to the brake, was never still for a moment. It was beyond him to comprehend that Tia was in complete control, not only of the minibus but of the oncoming traffic, causing it to slow, stop, or turn away.

The Earthquakes, used to Tia's ways by now, were enjoying every minute of it and making it a nightmare for Mr. Yokomoto by forever shouting advice: "Faster —faster!" "Look out for that guy!" "Climb over that

119

one!" or "Cut him off! Cut him off!"

In desperation Mr. Yokomoto finally screamed, "Shut up! Be quiet! Can't you see I'm concentrating?"

Presently the city was behind them and the minibus was roaring through the hills. As it reached the crest of a long hill, Rocky suddenly yelled to the others and pointed.

"There it is!" he cried. "The ball! The big ball!"

It was the great round dome of the reactor of the plutonium plant.

The minibus was making a terrible racket as it tore down the last stretch of the road to the gate. Cars and trucks and hastily moving people were leaving the plant, but only one vehicle was entering the gate. This was an armored truck. It was being admitted by a guard who was standing where the gatehouse had been earlier.

Just before they reached it, the armored truck drove through, and the gate was lowered. The guard stood behind it and signaled them to stop.

Mr. Yokomoto began kicking frantically at the brake while he struggled to turn the wheel.

Tia cried, "Keep going!"

She energized the gate, which started to rise. The guard grabbed it and tried to hold it down, but it continued to go up, carrying him with it. The minibus sped under him, headed for the reactor.

• • •

In the furnace room of the plutonium plant, while evacuation was beginning outside, the meter indicated that the temperature had risen dangerously close to the

120

red line. Dr. Gannon ignored it while he spoke over the telephone to the chief of staff.

"You say you've scraped two million together?"

"That's what I said," Mr. Clearcole replied. "Two million."

"Good start," said the doctor. "Now you've only got three more to go and fifteen minutes to do it in."

Letha Wedge, who was standing nervously by with Sickle, suddenly interrupted him. "Victor, it's terribly hot in here—and two million sounds terribly good to me. Why don't we take it?"

Dr. Gannon said coldly, "Five million is *terribly* better. I don't compromise. Do you hear me, Mr. Clearcole?"

"I hear you! Now you listen to my engineer."

A new voice on the telephone said, "If it doesn't start cooling in a very few minutes, there'll be a chain reaction, then everything—"

"Hear that?" Mr. Clearcole cut in. "We're just about at the point of no return. Another truckload has just come in, and now we have three and a half million dollars here in the control room. The balance is on the way."

"Call me when you've got it all," Dr. Gannon said.

"Wait a minute!" the chief of staff begged. "We're almost redlining! In less than ten minutes this place will be a hole in the ground!"

Dr. Gannon hung up. Above him in the control room Mr. Clearcole looked grimly at the dead phone in his hand, then hung it up. His hand balled into a fist and he slammed it down on his desk in anger and frustration.

121

"Evacuate everyone!" he ordered. "Call the governor and the mayor. Now I want volunteers for a skeleton crew to stay on a short while . . ."

• • •

Outside, after Mr. Clearcole had given the final evacuation order, there was sudden frantic activity. In the midst of this the minibus came screeching and spinning to a halt. As the motor choked off with a loud bang, everyone jumped away as if it, too, was on the point of exploding.

Tia and the Earthquakes piled out and raced into the building, followed by an unhappy and bewildered Mr. Yokomoto.

In the control room Tia ran into a worse frenzy than she had found outside. The desks were piled with money that men were madly counting. Others were running back and forth with papers in their hands or shouting over the telephones.

Mr. Clearcole, seeing her and the Earthquakes, snapped to the captain of the guard, "Get those sightseeing kids out of here! This is no time—"

"Sir," said Tia, "the people who are trying to destroy the reactor have kidnapped my brother. If I could see him, I might be able to stop them."

"She can do it!" the Earthquakes said together.

"You bet she can!" Mr. Yokomoto added, then gave his head a little shake and murmured, "Do what?"

The chief of staff looked grimly at Tia and said, "Impossible! They're inside the furnace room, and they've sealed the door somehow."

"What part of the reactor has to be fixed?" Tia asked.

"The emergency cooling system."

"Where is it?"

"Five levels down," he told her. "But it's almost too late. We're evacuating the plant in a minute or two." He turned away from her and barked to a uniformed man with a sack, "Put that money on the table!"

Tia looked quickly around, located the elevator, ran to it, and pressed the button. The Earthquakes followed close behind. At the sight of them she bit her lip and shook her head.

"You'd better leave," she said.

"Naw!" they said, almost as one. "We're stickin' with you!"

The elevator door opened and they poured into it.

Seeing them, Mr. Yokomoto cried, "Come back here!" He rushed to the elevator, but the door closed in his face.

The elevator opened upon the furnace room corridor. Tia and the others ran out and rushed toward the steel door at the end. They failed to see Dolan, who was still stuck to the ceiling.

"Help me!" Dolan cried. "Get me down! Help!"

They stopped short and looked up at him. Rocky said, "Tony's here, all right."

Tia degravitated Dolan and lowered him carefully to the floor. The guard, greatly relieved, thanked them warmly, then said, "Er, where are you going?"

"In there," said Tia, indicating the furnace room.

"Oh, no!" said Dolan. "You can't go past this point without an I.D."

He held out his arms, blocking them. Tia shook her

head and levitated him back to the ceiling. Leaving him gasping and protesting, they ran under him to the door.

Tia quickly energized the big steel door. As it unsealed itself and swung open, she ran inside. At the frightening hum and the heat, the Earthquakes hesitated, then they pulled themselves together and followed. The door swung shut behind them.

Tia found herself on a catwalk looking down. Almost immediately she saw Tony below her.

"Tony!" she cried. "Tony!"

13

FURNACE ROOM

TIA'S sudden and entirely unexpected appearance came as a great shock to Dr. Gannon, who was the first to look up and see her. The unpleasant knowledge of what she was capable of doing held him momentarily speechless.

Then he gasped her name, and both Sickle and Letha Wedge turned to stare at her and the four boys with her.

"How did she get away?" Letha said in a tight voice.

The doctor had been holding the control unit near his mouth when Tia's name escaped from him. At the sound of it Tony automatically turned to face her, but he showed no sign of recognition. The inner Tony, however, gave a soundless yell of delight. *Good old Alfred!* he cried. *He found your friends! Now we'll beat these devils!*

Even though he knew it would be next to impossible to call to her with enough force to attract her attention, he was on the point of trying it anyway when he realized she was looking directly at him. Suddenly he could feel the impact of her mind as it was directed toward his captive self.

Tony, she began, speaking telepathically, *Tony, listen to me! I am your sister, Tia, and those people you are with are our enemies. They've put us in great danger! You must break away from them, quickly, and run to the door! Tony!*

She was beginning to get through, for suddenly the inner Tony could feel signs of indecision and turmoil within his captive self. Immediately, with all the force he could muster, he began adding his own thoughts to Tia's. *Do what she says!* he ordered. *They are our enemies! Break away from them! Run for the door—Now!*

With a little more time it might have worked. But Dr. Gannon realized what was happening, slipped behind the switchboard, out of Tia's sight, and spoke hurriedly into the control unit.

"Tony," he ordered, "from this moment you cannot hear Tia. She cannot break through my power control. Acknowledge."

Turmoil ceased within the captive Tony, and he became a mindless wooden figure again. "Yes, sir," he said.

The inner Tony groaned and almost collapsed from the effort he had made. He had acted a little too soon. There will be another chance, he assured himself. He had better save his tiny speck of energy and not turn it on till he was absolutely sure of the moment.

Dr. Gannon called Sickle and Letha over to the safety area behind the switchboard.

"Get those kids!" he told them. "Fast!"

"But—but that awful little monster of a Tia," Letha protested. "She'll do those molecule things to us!"

126

"I'll take care of Tia before she gets a chance to. You two get the others."

As Letha and her nephew started up the stairs, Tia resolved to make another attempt to get Tony's attention. Desperately, and with all the power she could summon, she called to him again as she had before: *Tony, you've got to listen to me! I'm Tia. Try to remember me. Try to remember Witch Mountain! Try to remember the planet of the two suns!*

There was not the slightest response to her plea.

Her frustration changed quickly to fright, for she was all too conscious of the swift passage of time. Her hands clenched as she turned to the Earthquakes.

"I can't get through to him," she told them hurriedly. "I don't know what they've done to his mind. We'll have to find the emergency cooling system ourselves. It'll be down below somewhere."

"How do you spell cooling?" Rocky asked, as they ran along the catwalk to the stairs.

Before she could answer him, they were at the turn of the stairs, and suddenly they were confronted by Letha Wedge and her muscular nephew. Tia flashed past them without trouble, for it was obvious that neither of them wanted to run the risk of touching her. But with the Earthquakes it was an immediate scramble, punctuated by yells and swinging fists and furious kicks to adult shins. In seconds they were free and following Tia out upon the furnace room floor.

"Find the emergency switch!" Tia cried, and they scattered in all directions, searching even while Letha and Sickle came angrily after them.

Dr. Gannon, from his hiding place, watched her with growing concern as she stopped to look at a switchboard. Suddenly he spoke into his control unit, "Tony, we must eliminate Tia—now! You will cause the portable utility panel to run her down!"

In instant obedience to the murderous command, the captive Tony turned to a ponderous four-wheeled utility panel and sent it rolling swiftly in Tia's direction.

At the same moment the inner Tony, realizing the futility of attempting to stop the action in time, cried out a warning: *Tia! Tia! Watch out! Watch out!*

Something in his cry must have reached her, for Tia, intent upon her search for the switch, suddenly turned and saw the heavy panel bearing down on her. She managed to sidestep it, but it whirled and followed her. When it was only a few feet from her she again sidestepped it and was able to de-energize it. The panel swerved aside and struck the steel wall with a thunderous crash, scattering parts and fittings over the furnace room floor.

Tia's fear rose dangerously close to panic when she glimpsed the temperature meter and saw that the needle had reached the red line and was now creeping above it. Beyond it, steam was beginning to hiss in frightening clouds from a bank of pressure valves.

Across from Tia, Crusher was running past a panel that was clearly marked EMERGENCY COOLING SYSTEM. He stopped and came back and stared at it, frowning. Then he turned quickly and grabbed Rocky, who was running by. "What's that sign say?" Crusher asked.

Rocky looked hard at it. "No smokin'?"

"I—I better get Tia!"

128

Crusher spun about, saw Tia across the room, and yelled, "Tia! C'mere!"

She raced over. He pointed to the panel and said, "That ain't it, right?"

"You found it!" Tia exclaimed.

"I knew that was it!" Crusher said. "Only they got it spelt wrong."

Tia hardly heard him. Hands clenched, she was already concentrating on it. Re-energized, the switches unlocked and clicked on. Immediately the coolant began to flow.

Up in the nearly deserted control room, the monitor was hurriedly getting ready to leave with the last of the volunteers who had remained on duty. He started out, paused, and glanced back for a final look at the console. At that moment the console panels suddenly lighted up.

"Cooling system's on!" he yelled.

Down in the furnace room Dr. Gannon, still crouched in his place of safety well out of sight of Tia, saw the cooling system lights come on at the same time.

He swore, the first sign that his iron control was slipping, and spoke tersely into the microphone of his unit, "Tony, switch the cooling system off again!"

Tony did an about-face and stared at the distant panel. The switches clicked off.

Up in the control room the monitor put his hands to his head and groaned. "We've lost it again!" Everyone groaned with him.

Tia was still standing near the panel when it happened. She saw Tony, across from her, staring at it, and turned instantly and saw that the lights were out. Immediately she re-energized the switches. The lights came on and once again the coolant began to flow.

Upstairs there were sudden cheers, but down in the furnace room there was mad activity while the Earthquakes continued to dodge and fight off their disheveled and angry pursuers, who could not move nearly as fast. Dr. Gannon was in a fury.

Cursing, eyes flicking desperately from one piece of equipment to another, he settled on a heavy transformer a few yards to one side of Tia. She had to be disposed of, and quickly.

"Tony," the doctor rapped into his control unit, "you've got to get her this time—without fail! Levitate that transformer to the left of her and hit her with it! Hit her hard!"

Tony's gaze turned dutifully in the direction of the particular transformer, for there were others on the floor, and energized it. As it began to rise, the inner Tony gave another silent cry of warning: *Tia! Tia! Watch out behind you!*

Tia swerved around, saw the thing rising, and instantly levitated another transformer near it. She caused the two units to collide in midair.

Dr. Gannon, by now in a dangerous state of frustration, watched the things smash together and litter the floor with scrap. He cursed furiously, then his eye lighted upon a half dozen steel pipes on the floor beyond the wreckage of the transformers. "Those pipes, Tony," he ordered. "Throw them at her! Spear her with them! And don't you miss!"

Tony levitated the pipes and sent them flying toward Tia.

She saw them coming and hurriedly energized a

metal cabinet door and held it like a shield. With it she managed to deflect the pipes and send them clanging against the wall. Letha Wedge narrowly missed being brained by one while trying to corner Muscles.

From his hiding place Dr. Gannon peered cautiously out at Tia and cursed. For the first time since his discovery of Tony, he was beginning to regret that he had ever met the boy, not to speak of making a captive of him. Who would have dreamed that there would be a sister with the same incredible powers, a frail little person who probably could hold her own with the mightiest man on earth! It was frightening to realize what she could do to him. In a matter of seconds, if the chance came, she could wreck all his plans and put an end to his career as a scientist. But she mustn't be given that chance. Somehow he must put an end to her, and very quickly.

His eyes, desperately searching, glanced upward and saw the big gantry crane with a heavy load of steel plates suspended from it. That will do it, he told himself. But it will have to be handled in a different way this time. There should be a plan. . . .

Suddenly his jaws knotted with decision, and he spoke into the control unit, "Tony, listen very carefully. You will now pretend to remember Tia, understand? You will talk to her . . . lure her to the center of the room. Then you will cause the crane to drop its cargo on her. Is that clear?"

Tony, his face as cold and devoid of expression as a robot's, gave a mechanical nod.

"Good!" said the doctor. "Now call to her!"

Immediately Tony's expression changed. A confused

smile softened his face. He put his hands to his head as if it ached.

"Tia . . . ," he began.

Tia spun about and looked at him hopefully. "Tony?"

Tony took a few steps toward her and said hesitantly, "I—I'm starting to remember you . . . Tia . . ."

Tia moved forward a few paces. "Your voice sounds so strange, Tony. What's the matter with you?"

"I—I don't know . . . exactly. But I—I need your help."

"I came here to help you," she said. "You'll be all right now."

From his hiding place Dr. Gannon whispered into the control, "Tell her to come closer to you."

Tony held out his hands helplessly to Tia. "Take my . . . hand, Tia," he said uncertainly, his voice weak. "Get . . . me out of here."

Tia started toward him anxiously. When she was directly under the load, Tony said, "Stop there! Don't come any closer!"

The inner Tony cried, *Go back! Go back! You're in danger!*

Tia stopped, not immediately aware of the tiny voice within her mind. "Why?" she said. "What's wrong?"

"Er . . . because of the radiation."

"But radiation isn't a problem with us." Tia frowned and studied him suspiciously.

Dr. Gannon whispered quickly into the control, "Drop it on her, Tony!"

The captive Tony's eyes flicked upward. He energized the load. The inner Tony fairly screamed, *Watch it! There's danger overhead!*

132

This time the tiny voice reached her. She glanced up just as the heavy load began to drop.

Tia quickly counteracted the energy and the load came to a sudden stop, inches above her head. It seemed to float there in the air, belying its tremendous weight.

The suspense and uncertainty were all at once more than Dr. Gannon could stand. Abruptly he sprang from his hiding place. "Crush her, Tony!" he ordered hoarsely. "Exert a force greater than hers! Crush her! Crush her!"

The heavy load started downward again as Tony re-energized it. But the inner Tony was pounding furiously away in his skull: *No! No! Stop it! Stop it!*

Again and again the furious pounding was repeated: *No! Stop it! Stop it! No! No! Stop it!*

It seemed to have no effect at first, for Tia was quickly forced to her knees and began trying desperately to scramble away while she sought to bring the load to a stop. Then, of a sudden, the load wavered and grew light. Glimpsing Tony, she was startled by the look of confusion on his face. He seemed to be struggling against conflicting orders.

Beyond him, at the same moment, she saw Dr. Gannon and heard him shout angrily into his control unit, "Finish her, Tony! Finish her now!"

That one quick glimpse was all she needed to realize what the control unit was. Instantly she concentrated on it.

The thing suddenly crackled amid a shower of sparks, and smoke shot from it.

The doctor dropped it.

The load came down, pressing Tia to the floor.

14

TURNABOUT

IN THE BRIEF SECOND Tia had taken her attention from the load, it had slipped down until the cable holding it to the gantry crane had used up its slack and tightened. Even so, she managed to stop it before it pressed too close. Now, without Tony's power to fight, she sent it easily on the rise just as the Earthquakes came to pull her out from under it.

"You—you all right, Tia?" asked a frightened Muscles as he helped her to her feet.

"I'm all right," she said, looking anxiously around for Tony.

She saw him across the room, not far from Dr. Gannon. The doctor was scrambling about on hands and knees, trying vainly to overtake the control unit which was hopping around like a frog, giving off smoke and sparks. She raced to Tony, who was staggering blindly in a circle, hands over his ears as if he were in pain.

"Tony!" she cried, spinning him around. "Tony—look at me!"

"Tia . . . Tia . . . ," he said weakly in his misery. "Where—where are you? They hurt . . . They hurt!"

134

His unsteady hands were fumbling behind his ear. She looked quickly at the back of his head and saw the receptor. With a little gasp, she concentrated on the enslaving mechanism. It detached itself and fell to the floor.

Tony's agony stopped. He opened his eyes and looked at her while he slowly rubbed his forehead. He was himself again.

"Tia!" he managed to say at last. "What—where—how did you—"

"I'll bring you up to date," she said, and put her hands over his ears. An instant telepathic communication took place. He saw everything that had happened to her from that moment, ages ago, when he had left her at the taxi after it had run out of gas.

"What a time you had!" he exclaimed.

"What a time *you* had!" she said. "Alfred told me there was a part of you that—that—"

"That was sort of bottled up inside of me and escaped control. I could see most of what was going on, but I couldn't do much about it."

"I think you did a lot about it," she told him gratefully.

"I couldn't stop the other part of me from doing the things it did," he said. "All I could do was sort of slow it down." He closed his eyes and took a deep breath. "Anyway, it's sure great to be whole again!"

He opened his eyes and saw Dr. Gannon scampering after the elusive and still sparking and smoking control unit. The hate he had felt earlier rose again. He could easily have flipped the man off his feet and smashed him against the wall, but unlike the doctor, he did not come from a race of killers. Instead he concentrated on the control unit and caused it to stop. When the doctor pounced upon it, Tony made it blow to pieces with a flash and a black cloud of smoke.

Dr. Gannon, face blackened, staggered to his feet. His mouth twisted in anguish as he looked at the complete wreckage of his prized unit.

"Tony," he pleaded, struggling for speech. "Tony, please. . . . It isn't too late! We—we can still make use of molecular control!"

Tony pretended to think it over. "Okay, Doctor," he said finally. "Let's do it!"

He levitated Dr. Gannon in a series of somersaults upward to the end of the gantry crane and flipped him upon a small lifting platform suspended by wires from a hook. Though fairly safe, it was a frighteningly unstable seat, and the doctor clung to the wires with a death-defying grip, looking down fearfully and begging hoarsely for help.

Tia clapped her hands and said, "Oh, doesn't he look lovely up there?"

"He really does!" Tony agreed. "Now, if he just had some company . . ."

At that moment Letha Wedge came triumphantly around the corner of the reactor with Rocky and Crusher in tow. She was holding each boy painfully by an ear.

"Well," she began happily, "I've got these two brats . . ."

Then her mouth fell open and she stopped dead at the sight of Tia and Tony. A sound overhead made her look upward. She gasped to see Dr. Gannon on the platform. A sick imitation of a smile spread across her face. She released the ears in her hands and patted Rocky and Crusher affectionately on the head.

"Why don't we all go and have some ice cream," she said in a falsely gay voice. "Yes, some ice cream and soda and cake and . . . oh . . . oh . . ."

That was as far as she got, for abruptly she was levitated head over heels to the platform and deposited beside Dr. Gannon.

The doctor glared at her and said angrily, "Next time, I'll—"

"Forget it!" Letha snapped, as she clung fearfully to the wires. "I've lost my faith in science. Completely!"

No one noticed Sickle at this moment. The Earthquakes were getting acquainted with Tony, while Sickle, with the obstinacy of the muscle-bound, was creeping around the edge of the reactor on the lower catwalk. Suddenly he launched himself forward in one final desperate leap, evidently with the intention of capturing both sister and brother and thus saving the day. But it was not to be. Both Tony and Tia sensed his coming, and in the next second the incredulous Sickle was sent flying across the room to the platform, where he was deposited between Letha and the doctor. One glance over the side brought on an instant attack of acrophobia. He made a squealing sound like a dying goose, curled up in a ball, and clung like a leech to the platform.

Letha, with a look of annoyance at Sickle, sniffed and said, "It's absolutely dreadful the way they're bringing up children these days." She shook her head sadly.

Tia energized the big steel door. It swung open and Mr. Clearcole, a half dozen members of the security force, and little Mr. Yokomoto rushed into the furnace room.

They stopped in front of the Earthquakes, looked wildly around, then caught sight of the three disheveled and unhappy occupants of the high platform.

"There they are!" shouted the chief of staff, pointing a heavy finger at them. Then he yelled, "What are you doing up there?"

Dr. Gannon shouted down, "Those are the two who did it! Those kids, Tia and Tony! They're responsible for it all. They control molecular flow! They're way ahead of us!"

Mr. Clearcole looked at Tia and then at Tony. He shook his head. "Those quack scientists love to make important-sounding statements. Control molecular flow!" He gave a short laugh. "Here we work with atoms and molecules every day, and we all know how impossible it is. In fact, you probably don't even know what I'm talking about."

Tony and Tia glanced at each other, and shrugged innocently.

Mr. Yokomoto said, "I hope these truants haven't caused any trouble."

"They merely saved everything," said Mr. Clearcole, studying them curiously. "By the way, how *did* you do all the things you did?"

Tia gave him a nice smile. "I guess the molecules were on our side."

"You guess the molecules were"—Mr. Clearcole laughed a bit nervously—"on your side." He laughed

138

again. "I see . . ." Then in a low voice to Mr. Yokomoto he said, "What's she talking about?"

The truant officer shrugged. "I've got a couple questions myself, I'm afraid to ask."

The Earthquakes had surrounded Tony and were shaking his hand.

Rocky said, "You're tough, man."

"You're gonna take over this town," Muscles told him.

Crusher said, "We wanna join your gang."

"But I don't have a gang," Tony replied.

"You do now!" said Dazzler.

Tia said, "Tony, it's Friday. We have to meet Uncle Bené. And we have to pick up a friend along the way."

Mr. Yokomoto said, "I'd like to have a few words with your uncle, to get you kids straightened out."

• • •

On the way back in the minibus, they stopped at Letha Wedge's mansion and picked up Alfred, who was obviously glad to see them. By the time they reached the distant Rose Bowl, the Earthquakes had decided he should become a member of the gang, to which Alfred agreed with a hearty baa.

Outside the stadium the minibus chugged to a jerking, wheezy stop, choking off with a final bang that sounded as if the poor vehicle had come to the end of its last mile.

Everyone climbed out and looked at it sadly. Mr. Yokomoto's sadness was beyond words.

Tia whispered to Tony, "The bus won't run without

me in it. They'll be stranded here. And it's my fault it's such a mess."

"Then we'd better fix it," said Tony. "I'm sure it'll be okay with Uncle Bené. I'll do a motor job, and you do the bodywork."

They turned and concentrated on the minibus, energizing it.

A transformation began to take place. Slowly the crinkled metal began to uncrinkle and flatten out. Torn areas welded themselves together. Scratched and marred enamel smoothed over and gleamed like new again. Motor parts were magically repaired and reassembled. Presently the minibus was restored to its original condition. When the motor was started, it ran as smoothly as if it had just come from the factory.

Mr. Yokomoto and the Earthquakes watched the restoration with wonder and amazement.

Crusher whispered, "What a family!" and Mr. Yokomoto trotted around and around the gleaming machine, inspecting it, elated and confused. "What's going on here?" he said. "I *don't* understand."

Tony said, "The molecules must have rearranged themselves, somehow."

"That's a possibility," Mr. Yokomoto admitted.

Tia and Tony shrugged and smiled at him, and Mr. Yokomoto went on, "You know what this means? They never saw the wreck. I'll tell them the reports were exaggerated. . . . And if you kids would come back to school—especially after we've averted that disaster—I'm sure they won't fire me. You'll come back, won't you?"

The Earthquakes shifted uneasily from one foot to

the other. Muscles said, "If we was to go to school, . . . could we get to be as smart as Tia and Tony?"

"Maybe even smarter," Tia said.

"Well," said Dazzler, scowling, "let's give it a shot."

The others acted as if they were about to throw up, but reluctantly agreed.

"Great!" said Mr. Yokomoto. "I only hope the school can take it."

He climbed happily aboard the minibus to continue his inspection. Tony and Tia and the others ran toward the stadium, followed by Alfred.

When they reached the big gate, Tony said, "Open it, Tia."

"No," she said. "Everybody join hands."

Tony caught her look and grinned. When they had all joined hands, they levitated over the gate, the Earthquakes squealing with fright and delight. Alfred, left on the other side, baaed unhappily.

Tia said, "Oh, Alfred, come on!" She levitated him over the fence and was rewarded with a happy baa and a telepathic, *Thanks! That was great!*

Their craft was parked on the fifty-yard line, and as they reached the field they could see Uncle Bené standing in the glow under the cabin portal, waving.

The Earthquakes stopped in sudden fright.

"Wow!" Rocky gasped. "A flying saucer!"

"Take it easy," Tony said. "It's ours."

An awed Crusher said, "These kids have everything!"

"Will—will we ever see you again?" Muscles managed to ask.

"Maybe," said Tony. "Who knows?"

"Thanks for everything," Tia said, "and especially

141

for letting me be in the gang."

She gave each of them a good-bye kiss, which caused them to blush and squirm. Dazzler actually had tears on his cheeks.

Tia said, "Don't cry. We might come back soon."

"It's just that I—I don't wanna go to school," Dazzler managed to say. But he broke down and the others quickly pummeled him.

"Take good care of Alfred," Tia said finally. She gave him a good-bye kiss, then ran to the spacecraft with Tony.

Uncle Bené put his arms around them in a fond bear hug, and asked, "Where are your suitcases?"

"We lost them," said Tia. "There were a few problems."

"But did you have a good time?" Uncle Bené asked.

"Terrible," said Tony. "I knew we should have gone surfing."

They waved to the Earthquakes as they went aboard. Uncle Bené pressed the button that closed the cabin portal, and their craft rose easily with a soft humming sound. When it was well above the field it shot away and quickly vanished in the fog.

• • •

The Earthquakes and Alfred stood wide-eyed and breathless, staring at the sky until nothing could be seen. At last they started silently back the way they had come.

As they neared the fence, they stopped and looked at the big gate again.

Suddenly Crusher said, "Let's do it the way Tia and Tony taught us!"

They joined hands, ran at the gate, and jumped. All they managed to do was slam into the steel wire, bounce back, and crumple to the ground.

"Baa!" said Alfred, by way of laughter, and added for anyone to hear who could: *I could have told you it wouldn't work! You were born in the wrong world.*

In the parking lot, which they reached by the passageway, they rushed up to Mr. Yokomoto, who was still happily checking the minibus.

Muscles cried, "Yoyo . . . I mean, Mr. Yokomoto! Tony and Tia just took off in a flying saucer!"

Mr. Yokomoto raised his eyebrows. "A flying saucer?"

"Yeah!" Crusher exclaimed and imitated the saucer in sound and movement, "Whoooosh!"

"Whoooosh?" said Mr. Yokomoto, raising his eyebrows again. "How about whooshing yourselves into the bus?"

"But it's true!" Rocky cried.

Mr. Yokomoto shook his head. "I've seen those kids work miracles. I believe everything and anything—except that! Get in!"

Protesting, the Earthquakes climbed into the minibus, followed by Alfred.

Rocky said, "I hope that school teaches about flyin' saucers."

As the minibus pulled away, the Earthquakes stuck their heads out of the windows, looking upward. Suddenly they pointed and began waving excitedly.

High above them the spacecraft went through a break

143

in the fog. Tony and Tia were at a window, looking downward. For a moment they sighted the minibus moving like a tiny toy far below. They waved, and Tia sent a telepathic thought to Alfred: *Good luck, Alfred! We're going to miss you.*

She didn't expect a reply, but one came anyway. *Same here,* said Alfred. *I sure hope you come back soon!*

DATE		